John Francome, whose autobiography was a bestseller in 1985, has had an unrivalled career as a National Hunt jockey, enjoying not only astonishing success but also a vast popularity with the racing public. He has now set up as a trainer, and is already proving a success. EAVESDROPPER is his stunning debut as a writer of fiction.

James MacGregor is happily married and lives in London.

JOHN FRANCOME

& JAMES MACGREGOR

EAVESDROPPER

Futura

A Futura Book

ISBN 0 7088 3278 4

Reproduced, printed and bound in Great Britain by
Hazell Watson & Viney Limited,
Member of the BPCC Group,
Aylesbury, Bucks

Futura Publications
A Division of
Macdonald & Co (Publishers) Ltd
Greater London House
Hampstead Road
London NW1 7QX
A BPCC plc Company

Prologue

The horse box was empty and the only traces of life were the droppings on the straw which littered the floor. He cursed himself for believing that the tape would be handed over so easily. The eavesdropper plainly wanted revenge as well as money, but he would get neither. Damn the fellow. At least no one he knew had seen him walk across the field from the racecourse, let alone enter the vehicle, and if he hurried back now he could rejoin the others after the first race and say that his official business had ended early.

He peered ahead angrily, his senses quickening. Was that a noise he heard coming from the driver's cabin, or was it just his imagination playing tricks? Carefully he walked over to the bales of hay in the corner, climbed up and looked over the partition. Nothing. Only a discarded copy of *Horses in Training* on the torn leather passenger seat beside an empty packet of crisps.

'What the hell ... '

Someone had grabbed his arms from behind and was now holding them firmly behind his back.

He writhed and shouted, 'Let go you fool!'

But the grip only tightened as at the other end of the box someone closed the open door and began walking over towards them. For a moment there was darkness until his eyes adjusted to the faint gleam of light creeping through the window of the driver's cabin.

His attacker now pulled him down off the bales and in the struggle they wheeled round to face the still indistinct features of the new arrival. He managed to free himself just as he saw the gleam of the knife's blade lunging towards him.

In desperation, he tried to shield himself with the silk racing jacket he was carrying. The sharp point tore through it remorselessly on its path up and into his rib cage. He gasped with pain as the blade was twisted deeper and deeper.

A sudden jet of blood made his assailant jump back. In that brief moment, in the half light, he saw a face contorted with glee and venom. Incredulous, he swayed for what seemed an eternity before falling to the floor, his colours pinned to his chest as if in final tribute.

Chapter 1

'He then said that as far as he was concerned, the Jockey Club could bugger off.'

'He said *what*?' Sir Denby Croft, Senior Steward of the Jockey Club, the rulers of English racing, and acting chairman of its Disciplinary Committee, looked at Sir Guthrie Graves in anger and disbelief.

'That the Jockey Club could bugger off. I then told Mr Weatherby and young Kitson that having heard the evidence of the stipendiary steward and the racecourse vet my fellow stewards and I were not satisfied with their explanation as to the running of Gone Missing and that we were reporting them to the Disciplinary Committee in Portman Square.'

'And what was Mr Weatherby's reaction to that? A good deal more sensible, I hope?'

'Quite the contrary', Sir Guthrie answered. 'He replied, and I wrote it down at the time: "Those silly bastards couldn't spot a lame horse if it kicked them in the arse". '

It was obvious from the horrified expression on the committee members' faces that the enquiry now being held at No. 42 Portman Square, the Jockey Club's headquarters in London, was not veering in favour of leniency towards George Weatherby, Gone Missing's trainer, or his jockey Stewart Kitson. This was ironic. Weatherby had been suspected of cheating by the authorities for years yet on this occasion had been running a horse strictly on its merits. Kitson, usually an unscrupulous rider, had been genuinely trying to ride a winner. For once they had both been on the level. Their reward was to be in the dock.

The Woolridge Novice Selling Hurdle over two miles at Tadcaster had been Gone Missing's last chance to prove to an adoring and long-suffering owner that he could be first past the post otherwise than inside a greyhound. Normally, the race was won in a time not much faster than the donkey derby at Blackpool, and for this reason, and not because of any bet of George Weatherby's (he was too shrewd a punter for that) Gone Missing had started as co-favourite. For the first mile Kitson had no trouble in keeping him up with the leaders but it was when the field turned into the back straight and the race had started to hot up that disaster struck. As the runners crossed the road leading to the inside of the course and jumped the third last hurdle, Gone Missing had suddenly gone very lame. Kitson had had no alternative but to pull him up as quickly as possible, no mean feat with eighteen other runners to avoid.

Kitson was not completely surprised. Gone Missing had a history of leg problems which hefty vets' bills and endless prayers by the owner had failed to remedy, and now, it appeared £16,000-worth of training fees later, he had finally broken down. Having dismounted, the jockey began to lead his mount back to the stables, Gone Missing's head nodding with every painful step.

Then, just as they came over the brow of the hill in sight of the stewards' binoculars and looked down on the steep straight which leads to the last flight of hurdles, a seeming 'miracle' occurred and Gone Missing recovered his action. Once more he was as sound as a bell. Kitson realised that, instead of breaking down, the horse had just banged a nerve as he hit the fifth hurdle hard and now that the pain had gone, so had his lameness.

Leading a perfectly sound horse back to face a disbelieving owner and an anxious trainer is an embarrassment which most jockeys can do without, but in this instance, it had even more dire consequences for Kitson. He had hardly taken a dozen steps towards the weighing room with his saddle under his arm when the acting stipendiary steward collared him and said, 'Report to the stewards in five minutes. I've told Weatherby to be there as well.'

'What's wrong, sir?'

The acting stipendiary steward looked at him with contempt. 'As if you didn't know, Kitson. Your only trouble is, this time I've got you.'

Now six weeks later, at Portman Square, the acting stipendiary's prophecy was coming true. Sir Denby had the smell of blood in his nostrils, and was closing in for the kill.

'Well, Mr Weatherby, what explanation are you offering for your horse's performance?'

George Weatherby was a blunt Yorkshireman, direct in speech if not in motive. To him the sight of an old Etonian in full cry was like a red rag to a bull.

9

'The same explanation as I offered to Sir Guthrie and his cronies immediately after the race. Three fences from home the horse went lame. So Kitson – quite rightly in my opinion – pulled him up. The fact that he appeared sound after the race when the racecourse vet examined him has nowt to do with it. I ran that horse fair and square and nobody's going to say I didn't.'

'What evidence can you call to support your story?'

'Evidence? What bloody evidence do you require? You've already heard what Kitson told the local stewards, and any vet will tell you that this kind of thing is not uncommon. I suppose you want me to call the horse?'

'There is no need to be offensive, Weatherby. Unless you or Kitson have something useful to add, I must ask you to wait outside whilst we consider the evidence and reach our decision as to the proper penalty.'

Five minutes later, they were summoned back into the committee room. Sir Denby did not suggest that either culprit should be seated before launching into the verdict.

'We have listened to the evidence of Sir Guthrie Graves on behalf of the local stewards at Tadcaster and the explanation you have offered. We unanimously find the case proved against you. National Hunt racing must be protected from this kind of conduct. Horses must be allowed to run on their merits.' His voice had begun to rise hysterically. Now it calmed down again. 'Accordingly, we have decided that in your case, Weatherby, your licence to train shall be withdrawn for one year, with immediate effect, and that you, Kitson, shall forfeit your licence to ride for a similar period. We hope, Weatherby, that on reflection you regret the most unfortunate and offensive comments that you have made about the Jockey Club. Have either of you anything to say?'

Kitson merely shook his head sullenly. He remained staring vacantly into space, his reaction to the onslaughts of authority since his schooldays.

Weatherby, by contrast, shook his right fist in the air and started shouting. 'Aye, plenty. I haven't spent thirty years in racing to have it all ruined by the likes of you and this kangaroo court.'

'Control yourself, man,' interrupted the Senior Steward, 'or I'll ask the secretary to remove you!'

By the look on the secretary's face, it was not a prospect he relished.

'Control myself? You've got a bloody nerve! You just wait, Croft! Your turn will come, and it may be a damn sight sooner than you expect!' And with that, Weatherby stormed from the room.

The effect of Weatherby's outburst was short-lived. After calling the enquiry formally to a close, Sir Denby telephoned his wife, Clarissa, at their London flat and, as was his custom, told her in detail of what had occurred. She was outraged at the trainer's behaviour, and consoled her husband by pointing out that it was just what one would expect from a common little Northerner. As for his threats, they should be treated with the contempt they deserved.

Sir Denby put down the phone feeling greatly relieved. Marrying Clarissa after his first wife died had been the best thing he'd ever done, and her loyalty and understanding had certainly shown how wrong some of his friends had been to suggest she was only after his money. He was now able to attack his lunch and the excellent claret with even more than his usual gusto, and three hours later, after a short nap in his room, he decided to make the thirty-minute walk from Portman Square to Buff's, his other favourite club, at the top of St James's. Although it was still drizzling, he preferred his own company to that of some East End cab driver with his endless chatter about what was wrong with the world today. After all, the answer was simple. Shoot the lefties and reintroduce National Service. A dose of that would cure all ills.

Before crossing Piccadilly he made a short detour to Windrush and Son, suppliers of all things equine to the racing and hunting fraternity, to see if his new set of racing colours was ready. Clarissa had brought back the silk as a present from her recent trip to Hong Kong, and he was looking forward to seeing it worn on the racetrack. Gazing at the riding whips on display in the window, he was reminded of the large fines he had imposed at a recent enquiry on two young jockeys for excessive use of that implement in a photo-finish at Kempton. As far as he was concerned, that sort of thing was best left to the bedroom. Happily the new silks were ready and, having charged them to his account and waited for them to be wrapped, he set off again. Marching into Buff's his thoughts were on the large double Bloody Mary's which would soon restore him in the warmth of the members' bar. Nobody mixed them quite like Childers, the unsmiling, desiccated, eminently sober-looking wizard who had presided over the rites of the club's cocktail shaker for the past nineteen years – or was it the past twenty-nine? Cheered by the thought that some things at least never changed, Sir Denby sprang nimbly up the three stone steps of the entrance, pushed open the battered swing doors, gave his grey overcoat, bowler hat, umbrella and package to Groves, the hall porter, and wandered over to the club noticeboard.

He was reading the list of nominees for the Vintage Port committee when he spotted a letter with his name on it pinned to the green baize. The clumsy typing suggested that it was from the new french chef

12

enclosing the menu for next week's regimental dinner. Anxious to see what kind of fancy food was being proposed, he ripped it open.

The contents were anything but culinary. 'THE JOCKEY CLUB PUNISHES CHEATS. YOUR TURN IS NEXT, CROFT' The words had been cut from a newspaper and pasted onto a grubby sheet of cardboard.

Muttering under his breath in astonishment, Sir Denby stared at the note and then shouted for Groves.

'When did this letter arrive?' he bellowed at the aged club servant, waving the envelope and note in front of his face.

Groves strained to look at the contents, but Sir Denby quickly moved his hand away and stuffed the papers inside his jacket pocket. 'Get on with it, man!'

'About an hour or two ago, my lord.' To Groves, all members of the club were members of the British aristocracy, and in his fifty years of service, no one had ever sought to correct him.

'And who left it here?'

'One of those bike boys – you know the type, my lord with their radios blaring.'

Sir Denby did not know the type and did not wish to. With a wave of his hand, he sent Groves about his business. His initial incredulity was now giving way to anger. If this was a joke, he was not amused. If it was some kind of veiled threat, he was not a man to be tampered with. He had been a member of the Jockey Club since leaving the Guards, and the famous Croft colours were known on every racecourse. At the present time alone, he had six horses in training with the highly successful Archie Duncan at Lambourn. They included two of the most promising hurdlers now racing: Paradise Lost and Paradise Regained. Those names, chosen by Clarissa, had provoked considerable

13

teasing on the part of his county friends, particularly in Leicestershire, where the family seat was to be found. He thanked God that they had never discovered that the Jockey Club had refused to register They Also Serve Who Only Stand And Wait.

Cooling down slightly, he decided to dismiss the letter as the work of a maniac, and proceeded to the bar. It was empty for once, and having put Childers to work on his Bloody Mary he was left to his own thoughts. He gulped down Childers's first offering and ordered another. As he sipped it, he recalled a telephone conversation which he and Archie Duncan had had a month previously, the night before Paradise Lost was due to run in a handicap hurdle at Huntingdon.

It had long been his greatest wish to win the big hurdle race named in memory of his late father, Sir Oswald, and due to be run this year on Friday the 25th of November, the day before the Hennessy Gold Cup. A good performance at Huntingdon, or worst of all victory, would have had a disastrous effect on Paradise's handicap weight for the Newbury race. With that in mind, and for what he regarded as the best of motives, he had given Duncan instructions for the horse to have an easy race. It now occurred to him that Duncan might have said something indiscreet to the jockey. In itself this was unlikely. True, Duncan had only trained his horses for the past two years, but he was an old friend of Clarissa's and his reputation as a heavy gambler was a thing of the past. It was imperative for Denby that his trainer should be beyond reproach and even more so that he should be publicly seen as such. That was, after all, the reason he had taken his horses away from Duncan's leading rival, Morton Marsh, after the *Sportsman* newspaper had published an article accusing him of giving the occasional runner an artificial stimulant to go faster. Of

14

course Marsh had protested his innocence, and no doubt rightly so, but it just did not do to be associated with that kind of thing.

Still, he decided to give Duncan a call to make sure. If the trainer had been foolish and had implicated him, he was going to have some empty boxes in his yard in the morning.

Sir Denby went into the cubby-hole facing the porter's lodge where the coin-box telephone for the use of the members was placed. The trainer was at home.

'Duncan? Denby here.'

'Oh hello, Denby. Everything OK? I've just been supervising the evening feed. You'll be pleased to hear that Paradise is right as rain, and he'll be all set for the big one in two weeks' time.'

'Good. It's about Paradise I'm calling.'

'No problems, I hope?'

'No, not really. It's just that, er, you remember that little conversation we had before Huntingdon?'

'Of course. You told me to give him an easy race.'

'Not so loud, man, someone might hear.'

'Sorry, but there's nobody else here at the moment.'

'Did you say anything about me to the jockey?'

'You mean about the instructions? Of course not. I just told him that I wanted to try running the horse from the front to see whether he could stay two and a half instead of two miles. I knew he'd have no chance of winning, ridden like that.'

'Good.'

'There's no problem, is there?'

'No, none at all. I just wanted to avoid any weighing-room gossip. Could be awkward after Newbury.'

'Don't worry. If anyone complains after he wins, it'll be me, not you, who'll have to do the explaining.'

'Is there any news of the weights?'

'Yes. The handicap was published this morning. He's got 10st 6lbs, which by my reckoning means he can't be beat.'

'Excellent. This is one race that I do really want to win. Goodnight, Duncan.'

'Goodbye Denby.'

Sir Denby returned to the bar. By now the place had filled up and he found himself chatting with two members from the City, both keen racegoers and owners. He was in the middle of recounting the events of that morning's hearing at the Disciplinary Committee when Groves interrupted him.

'Telephone for you, my lord.'

'Oh? Who is it?' If there was one thing Sir Denby disliked, it was telephone calls at his club.

'I don't know, my lord. A man, but he didn't give me his name. Just said it was urgent and would I ask you to take the call.'

Fuming, Sir Denby descended the stairs and re-entered the tiny cubicle. He snatched the receiver. 'Yes? Croft here. Who is it?'

'Hello, Sir Denby.' The voice sounded flat and toneless, almost muffled. 'Quite a pleasure to be talking to you.'

'Who is this?' Sir Denby's voice was growing louder. He realised he had failed to close the door of the cubicle and slammed it shut.

'Don't worry about my name, Sir Denby. Just listen to this and see if it refreshes your memory.'

There was a short pause, a hiss, and then two voices in conversation. It was a recording of the telephone conversation on the night before the Huntingdon race. 'Archie, I'm not going to let the handicapper get in my way this time. I want you to give Paradise an easy race tomorrow.' 'Fine, that shouldn't be too difficult. It's further than his best distance and if we run him from

16

the front, instead of waiting with him, he'll have no chance. He'll blow up and nobody can criticise us.' 'All right. Be careful what you say to the jockey, though.' 'That's no problem. He'll do what he's told and I won't tell him very much.'

The recording stopped and the caller, his voice a shade more animated this time, but still curiously distorted, resumed. 'Who's been a naughty boy, then?'

'How dare you! I'll ... '

'Keep calm, Sir Denby, keep calm. There's no reason why this recording of your fine voice should get into the wrong hands.'

'This is blackmail. I will inform the ... '

'Not the police, I'm sure. Because if you do, Sir Denby, I'll tell you what'll happen. Copies will go to the Jockey Club, and you wouldn't like that, would you? And they'll go to all those nasty common newspapers. Just think of the publicity.'

Sir Denby did, and began to sweat.

'What do you want?'

'A fair price, but we can discuss that all in good time. Just you sleep on it and wait for me to get in touch.'

There was a click as the line went dead. Sir Denby held the receiver a few seconds longer, then slowly and gently put it back. He thought back to Weatherby's threats that morning and felt a mixture of emotions: fright, a most unusual condition for him; but also outrage, which was more comforting. After standing in the cubicle a minute or so longer — Groves, looking across from his lodge, was surprised to see him swaying slightly — he made up his mind. He wouldn't call the police. Those people had a dangerous habit of leaking things to the press and anyway he could not face the embarrassment of a trial, anonymity or no anonymity.

Nor would he worry Clarissa, nor involve Duncan. No, he was going to arrange to meet this would-be blackmailer, demand the return of the tapes, and what's more give him a piece of his mind. A fairly resistible gift, if he had only known.

Chapter 2

James Thackeray, racing journalist, tipster, amateur jockey and would-be *bon viveur*, was fast asleep as the racecourse commentator announced the weight changes for the Hartley Hurdle. When the race train from Paddington had arrived at its destination, the little station that adjoins Newbury racecourse, the other occupants of the carriage had grabbed their binoculars, TIMEFORMS and racing papers and gaily leapt onto the platform as if picking winners was a mere formality and the only problem was going to be how to carry home the winnings. They had paid little attention to the figure huddled in a thick, russet tweed overcoat, his brown curly hair falling over his forehead, who had dozed off in the corner over a grubby and obviously much travelled paperback soon after the train had idled out of London.

James was deep in his dreams and just about to undo the top button of Meryl Streep's blouse when the commentator somewhere in the distance asked the jockeys to mount. Those familiar words penetrated his subconscious and brought him back from his fantasy world to the land of the living. Still half asleep, he looked at his watch and realised that he was already ten minutes late for his meeting with Paddy Develera, a lad working in Monty Spry's racing stables at Compton. For a hundred pounds a year, happily paid for by James's employer, the *Sportsman* newspaper, Paddy, like several other lads up and down the country, supplied useful information about the chances of his governor's horses. The next day, Saturday 26th November, was the Hennessy Gold Cup, one of the big steeplechase races of the year, and as Monty Spry trained the second favourite the meeting could be informative. However, James was beginning to wonder whether Paddy was obtaining his information from the right part of the horse's anatomy, as his last two certainties had both finished in the ruck.

He crossed the bridge which led from the station to the racecourse and broke into an unsteady trot as he made his way to the field where all the horse-boxes bringing runners to that afternoon's races were parked. It was a bitterly cold autumn day and James's breath danced like smoke signals in the air ahead of him. He had not yet gone into serious training for his own riding after having a three-month lay-off through injury and the 14-odd pounds overweight which his body was carrying soon took its toll. By the time he had reached the field he was definitely wheezing. Puffing shamefully, he began to pick his way towards the furthest corner where Paddy had said Monty Spry's box would be parked. Why he couldn't speak to Paddy on the telephone he never knew, but the Irishman treated his role as an informer with deadly seriousness, and passed on the name of a fancied horse as if it was the formula for a secret cure for AIDS.

As he reached the blue-painted horsebox which bore Monty Spry's name on its side in bold red letters, James could hear the commentary on the first race. In his morning's selections he had tipped the likely favourite, The Cavalier, and from what he could gather the horse was already prominent. Unfortunately the same could not be said of Paddy. He knocked on the door of the horsebox and whispered his name, just in case the careful Irishman was taking his role as undercover agent to its full limits. There was no reply and James cursed himself for being so late. He had not intended to get drunk the night before, but after a couple of glasses of champagne his judgement tended to take a sabbatical. He decided to make for the racetrack and a strong cup of coffee in the press room. After that he would go and hunt out Paddy, who could nearly always be found investing his wages in the betting shop in Tattersalls enclosure.

He had only walked about ten yards when he was stopped in his tracks. A hoarse voice, shaky from indignation and rage, grunted out the words 'Let go, you fool!' The sounds of a scuffle followed.

James stood still to listen. The horses in the first race were apparently coming to the last hurdle and judging by the roar of the crowd, the favourite was right there in contention. With so much noise going on James wondered whether his ears had deceived him. He fervently hoped so. He had never been particularly keen to involve himself in other people's disputes, especially when they became violent. The next sound, however, banished any such comforting thoughts. It was a low gasp of pain. Then a few seconds later came a thump, like a sack of potatoes hitting the floor. James knew that in the films the hero would now leap forward to find out what was happening. But what of the dangers of having a go? The newspapers were full of stories of people who had done this and paid the penalty.

Triumphing reluctantly over his fears, he finally rushed to one of the horse boxes from which he thought the noise might have come. He knocked on the door and when his rather feeble cry of 'Is anyone there?' went unanswered, tried the handle and found the door unlocked. With trepidation he pulled it open. The box was empty. Enormously relieved, and once more putting his experience down to what he hoped was merely the first stages of delirium tremens, he set off hurriedly for the entry to the members' enclosure.

As he rushed through the entrance gates, the sight of a policeman in uniform made him wonder whether he should at least report the incident. He decided to turn back and tell the officer what he had heard. The sceptical look on the policeman's face suggested that he thought James was mentally unstable and, if anything, he seemed even more convinced of his diagnosis when James announced that he was a journalist. It took a great deal of persuasion before he reluctantly agreed that they should go and investigate together.

There was only one trouble. James realised that he could not identify the source of the noise with any certainty. With a highly sceptical policeman in tow, he tried two or three boxes, all of which turned out to be locked.

'The trouble with you journalists,' the policeman observed sarcastically, 'is you're always looking for a story. Just too much imagination.'

By now some of the horses from the first race were being led back by their lads and curious glances were being cast in the two men's direction.

'I'm sorry, officer. I know it sounds ridiculous. But I did hear those noises and I'm certain they came from one of these boxes.'

'Yes, sir, but which one? Can't you be a little more definite?'

'It was all over so quickly. As I told you, the only one I looked in was empty.'

At this moment the door of an extremely dirty, once cream-coloured box blew open in the wind and then slammed shut again.

'Let's try that one,' said James.

The officer gave him that indulgent look normally reserved for old ladies who report their cats missing. Together they walked the twenty yards towards the box. On the back of the twin doors were painted the words:

George Weatherby

Racing Stables

Malton

James went to open the right hand door but the officer pulled him gently to one side.

'I think I ought to be the one to discover the body, sir,' he said jeeringly, a wide grin on his face. He peered inside. All that could be seen in the overcast light were several bales of hay piled in the corner behind the driver's cabin.

'Looks like there's nothing there, sir,' he said, turning to James. 'Have a look for yourself.'

Feeling relieved, James peered inside. Nothing. 'Perhaps you ought to look right inside, officer, just to make sure,' he said.

The policeman's expression made it plain that he had had his fill of his companion's antics. However, he climbed inside and walked over to the bales of hay in the corner. James tiptoed behind him.

'As I thought. Nothing … Jesus Christ!'

James rushed forward at the startled tone of the officer's voice. There, lying in the corner, partly obscured by the bales of hay, was the body of a man in a tweed suit and grey overcoat. His face and the top part of his chest were draped with a yellow silk racing jacket. Neatly resting at a rakish angle on the top of his head was a purple riding cap. A knife was protruding through the jacket and the yellow around it was slowly turning scarlet. The man was clearly dead.

'I think this is my job, sir,' the policeman said, gently but firmly pushing James behind him as they approached the grotesque corpse. Without worrying about fingerprints, he folded over the yellow jacket and lifted up the purple cap. The eyes of a middle-aged man stared up at them in fixed incredulity, his flabby jowls spilling over a stiff white collar from which emerged the knot of a regimental tie.

'Good God!' said James. 'Surely ... it can't be ... '

'You know him then, sir?' the policeman asked suspiciously.

'Know him? Who on the racecourse doesn't? That, officer, is none other than the Senior Steward of the Jockey Club.'

'And who's he, when he's at home?'

'Sir Denby Weatherington Makepeace Croft, to give him his full name.'

It was then that James spotted a crumpled piece of paper on one of the bales of hay behind Sir Denby's head. He bent down and picked it up and, without looking at its contents, handed it to the officer.

'This might be of importance,' he suggested respectfully.

The officer snatched it from him. 'I'd prefer if you didn't touch anything, sir.' He opened it up to reveal what looked like a betting slip with several typed selections on it and James edged closer for a proper look. But the policeman quickly folded it again and slipped it inside a compartment at the back of his notebook. 'I think you had better come with me whilst I go for further assistance.'

James was delighted with the invitation, as he had no desire to wait on his own beside the Senior Steward's body.

Fifteen minutes later he was back in the horse box, and this time he found himself on the receiving end of a number of hostile questions from a certain Inspector Hardcastle, the most senior officer on duty at the course. A dirty old horse blanket was now covering the corpse.

'Please tell me again, Mr Thackeray, what you say you were doing here in the first place.'

'As I've told you, Inspector, and I'm sure your assistant wrote it down the first time, I had arranged to meet a stable lad called Paddy Develera beside his boss's horsebox half an hour before the first race. Mr Develera supplies me with information about the chances of his boss's horses.'

'Do you usually meet in such strange places?'

'Invariably. Paddy goes in for the cloak and dagger bit.'

James winced at his somewhat unfortunate choice of words in the company of the dead man. 'And who am I to ruin his fantasies?'

'When did you arrange this meeting, then?'

'Last night. Tomorrow is the Hennessy Gold Cup, which, as you no doubt know, is one of the big races of the season, and Paddy's boss, Monty Spry, trains the second favourite. I hoped Paddy, who looks after the horse, might be able to tell me how well he was.'

'So what happened to this Mr Develera?'

'I suspect he got bored with waiting. He can't resist a bet and probably went off to put his wage packet on the first race.'

'Why did you say you were late?'

'I told you. I had a heavy night and fell asleep on the race train.'

'Did anyone see you there?'

'I doubt it. I certainly didn't recognise anybody in my compartment and I very much doubt if my fellow passengers paid any attention to me. They would almost certainly be thinking about the racing and what they were going to back.'

'How long did you look for him?'

'About two or three minutes. I was just giving up when I heard the noises, and you know the rest.'

'Do we? No doubt we shall see. That's all for the moment, Mr Thackeray. You can go and watch the racing, but I want you to come and see me again in the Chief Security Officer's room under the grandstand in half an hour's time. In the meantime, don't tell anybody on the course what happened, is that clear?'

'Perfectly. Aren't you going to tell the old boy's wife? They've got a runner in the fourth, the big race named after his father.'

'When's that?'

'In about a quarter of an hour.'

The inspector looked at his watch and thought for a moment. 'I don't see any point in upsetting her just yet. I'll break the news after the race. That doesn't mean I want you telling her. You can go now.'

Just as James was leaving the inspector called him back. 'Mr Thackeray, do you know anything about this man Weatherby?'

'He's a trainer. Or more accurately, he *was* a trainer until two weeks ago. Sir Denby took away his licence for a year for not running one of his horses straight.'

The inspector's face lit up. James reflected that it was a good job he hadn't mentioned the rumour of

Weatherby's threats. 'So what would he be doing on the racetrack?'

That was a question James had already asked himself. 'He's still entitled to come and watch, only not to train horses under rules.'

'In which case, why would he bother to bring his horse box with him and all the way from Malton?'

James just shook his head. 'You'll have to ask him. I'm sure there's some innocent explanation.'

'I'm going to, and for your sake, I hope there isn't, otherwise you'll have a great deal more explaining to do. See you later.'

James rushed back to the course, as he was anxious to watch the Sir Oswald Croft Memorial Handicap Hurdle. It was going to be a rather curious sensation watching Sir Denby's horse run when its owner lay lifeless in the corner of a muddy field, but James' interest was not solely ghoulish. He had napped The Teaser in preference to Paradise Lost and was desperately in need of a winner to boost his position in the Naps Competition, organised by a rival racing paper for racing journalists. There was talk of redundancies at work, and he was anxious to establish himself as a man in form.

Passing a call box he decided to phone the *Sportsman*'s office. He could not risk being overheard in the press room. The inspector had forbidden communication to anyone on the racecourse, so all James felt he was doing was taking him at his literal word. He was put through to his editor, Carlton Williams, who did not seem all that amused by the opening greeting of 'Hold the front page!', but immediately started speaking into the second telephone on his desk as James told him of his sensational discovery. James was ordered to return to the office as soon as the last race was over, instead of dictating his copy from the racecourse press room.

Reaching his favourite viewing spot on the roof above the members' stand, just as the runners were approaching the fourth hurdle from home, James could pick out through his binoculars the colours of The Teaser going well in second place. About five lengths further back and going ominously easily was Paradise Lost. His jockey was wearing Sir Denby's second colours, identical to those which had draped his body, save for the addition of purple epaulettes.

As the horses came off the bend on the far side the pace quickened. Galloping downhill, some of the stragglers were having difficulty keeping up and not surprisingly three fell at the next flight. Neither The Teaser nor Paradise Lost were among them. James noticed how Paradise's jockey, the brilliant Phil Hope, had taken the precaution of pulling his horse a yard to the right just before the hurdle and then back to the left, so that he was jumping at an angle towards the inside of the course and could thus avoid being brought down by a faller.

The horses rounded the last bend for home. The Teaser was still going well and had now taken up the running, but jumping the third last and with only half a mile to run he was clearly beginning to tire. His jockey switched him from the inner to the stand side so that he could use the running rail dividing the flat from the hurdle course to help him gallop in a straight line.

As they approached the second last, The Teaser was now only two lengths up on Paradise. To James's dismay Phil Hope conjured an enormous leap out of the 7 to 1 chance and the roar of the crowd began to fade as Paradise ranged up beside the favourite at the last and then ran on to pass the post five lengths clear. Below him in the public enclosures James could hear the occasional jeer from angry punters.

Putting his own disappointment behind him, James rushed downstairs to join his press colleagues in the winning enclosure. There to greet the triumphant hurdler and his smiling jockey were its tall dapper trainer, Archie Duncan and beside him the elegant, fur-clad figure of Lady Croft. James reckoned that she was just the wrong side of forty, but with her hollow cheekbones and well-preserved figure she was by any standards an extremely attractive woman. It was obvious from her enthusiasm that she had no idea that she was now a widow. James wondered how she would react to the news, since word in the racing world was that they were a devoted couple.

He held back from asking any questions, but not surprisingly one of his colleagues asked where her husband was.

'He was called away on urgent business before the first race, and he's obviously been held up. I only hope he's been watching the race from the Stewards' room. He will be absolutely delighted with this win, that I can assure you.'

If only she knew, poor thing, thought James.

James was apprehensive as he walked to the Chief Security Officer's room where Inspector Hardcastle and two assistants were waiting. And he was right. He was subjected to another twenty-minute grilling and made to go through his story twice more. He could not tell from the inspector's taciturn expression whether he believed him or not.

'One last thing, Mr Thackeray. We've located Mr Develera, just where you said he was likely to be.'

'Oh good.' James perked up. 'He confirmed about our planned meeting, then?'

'Not exactly,' replied the inspector. 'In fact, when we

29

asked him if he had arranged to meet you, he looked rather furtive, and answered that he had never met you in his life. You might think about that, Mr Thackeray.'

James felt himself blushing as he left the room. Trust his luck to have picked on Ireland's answer to George Smiley.

Chapter 3

The last race was won by an outsider, Archimedes, at 33 to 1, making a double for Archie Duncan. James decided to miss out on the usual interview in the winner's enclosure with the victorious trainer. He felt embarrassed at the idea of questioning Duncan, the horse's trainer, about Archimedes's future race plans, when he was still unaware that his stable's best-known and biggest owner was no longer in any condition to pay his training fees. He chose instead to make straight for the 'spivs' special', as the race train was affectionately called.

He found himself sharing a compartment with three other men. On his side, and next to the door, sat a young fair-haired man in his thirties who already had the harrassed air of a compulsive gambler. He wore his

Barr and Stroud binoculars like a military sash across his raincoat and was submerged in the pages of that day's TIMEFORM racecard with its individual analysis and rating of each runner. Every now and then, with a knowing grunt, he marked one of the entries with his pen. A certain future loser, thought James.

The pair sitting opposite were bookmakers, James reckoned, judging by the fat leather satchels in the luggage rack above their heads and the contented smiles on their faces. He was proved right shortly after Reading.

'Had a good day, Joe?' asked the shorter one, who was sporting a very loud check suit.

'Not great. I had to pay up a bit on that favourite of Marsh's, but worst of all, I laid a thousand pounds to thirty Archimedes to some knowing sod. What about you, Ron?'

'All right, except for bloody Paradise. Should have been a steward's enquiry, if you ask me. Cost me a packet. If you'd seen the way it ran at Huntingdon last month.'

'Doesn't surprise me. I expect that geezer Croft wanted to win a race named after his old man. Trouble is, those buggers think they're above the law.'

'What do you mean? They *are* the law!' Ron roared with laughter at his own joke, and turned his attention to a copy of that day's *Sportsman*, which, until then, had been nestling in the right-hand pocket of his sheepskin overcoat.

Five minutes later, he put down the paper in disgust. 'Christ, that bloke Thackeray writes a load of rubbish!'

'James Thackeray?'

'Yes, that's him. He writes about as badly as he rides.'

'Never read his stuff myself. I'm told he occasionally tips a long price winner.'

'You'll find better tips at the end of a snooker cue!' Ron laughed again at this second sample of his own wit, while James blushed and kept his head down, pretending to be engrossed in his racing novel, and the hero's septic foot.

Twenty minutes after the train's arrival at Paddington, James was in the *Sportsman*'s offices in Fleet Street. He rushed immediately to see the editor. Carlton Williams had been editor of the *Sportsman* for fifteen years, and a journalist since Caxton invented printing. He was a cynic, but commanded the loyalty and respect of his staff.

After listening to James' detailed, if somewhat impetuous, account of the afternoon's sensational happenings he asked, 'How do you know it wasn't suicide?'

'At Newbury racecourse? In his own colours, and with a dagger in his heart?' James laughed nervously.

'Sounds more like a solution in Cluedo to me. He could have had money problems. Some of these upper-class blokes aren't so rich as they seem.'

'His only money problem was how to spend it. There were no children. Lady Croft is going to be a seriously rich widow. This was murder. The police are certain of it. And judging by the way they treated me, I'm one of their suspects.'

'Anyone else? What about this fellow Weatherby?'

'He certainly had every reason to hate Croft's guts. Two weeks ago the old boy took away his licence to train for a year for pulling a horse. But that's scarcely a reason for murder. A bit of overkill, if you'll forgive the pun.'

'I don't know, there have been occasions when I've felt like knocking off the odd sub, or come to think of it, racing tipster.'

Carlton grinned at James, who merely replied, 'Will

33

this be lead story tomorrow?'

'Maybe, but as it's the Hennessy Gold Cup, we normally like to splash our selection across the front page.'

'Who are we going for?'

'Man On The Run. Appropriate name in the circumstances.'

'But surely this is more important. It's not every day that a Senior Steward of the Jockey Club is murdered at Newbury racecourse.'

'Well, that's true, of course, but our readers have one-track minds. They want to back winners, not read about births, death or marriages, however gory. Now it if had been Man On The Run who'd been found dead in the car park ... '

James looked crestfallen.

'Don't worry. You write the article and I'm sure your pal the chief sub-editor will see what he can do. He terrifies me, but then subs always have. Just make sure that you fill it with a lot of the eye-witness stuff, with particular emphasis on the blood, and the grief-stricken widow. Oh, and tell the picture desk to get out a photo of Croft and caption it "In happier times". What else should you be telling me?'

'Only this. Sir Denby's horse Paradise Lost won the 2.30. By my reckoning his owner was dead at 1.10 at the latest. Jockey Club rules say that a dead man can't own a racehorse. So strictly interpreted, Paradise ought to be disqualified.'

'Now that's quite a thought. We might even work it into the headline. How about "Angry Punters Storm Mortuary"? ' Carlton gave one of his rare chuckles.

James went to his desk in the open-plan office and sat down by his typewriter. Although his mind was overflowing with the day's events he had difficulty in transmitting them in an intelligible form through his two fingers. Eventually, and with the bookmaker's hurtful remarks ringing in his ears, he managed to knock out a thousand words.

He walked over and handed his copy to the chief sub-editor. 'Make sure he leads with it.'

'I'll do my best, Jim boy!' came the reply.

James glanced at his watch. It was already 8 o'clock and he had arranged to meet an old flame, Julia Foss, in a bar off Jermyn Street at 8.15. It meant that he had no time to go back to his flat in Redcliffe Gardens to have a bath. She'd just have to put up with the authentic smell of the race track, an aroma as yet unattainable at any duty-free scent counter. Anyway, James reasoned, she was certain to go wild when she heard that he was a murder suspect. The best he could do was to borrow some deodorant from the office Romeo, Bob Hailey, on the results desk. Shortage of time meant that unfortunately he could not remove his shirt before application.

Three quarters of an hour later, he was still propping up the bar, and reflecting on his day over a large Bloody Mary, long on Worcester Sauce, shaken on ice, but with none in the glass. There was no sign of Julia. James was just about to resuscitate his flagging conversation with the barman, who, judging by his tight trousers, was more interested in modern dance than horse racing, when he felt a light tap on his shoulder.

'Are you James Thackeray?'

He turned to see a young girl, about five foot six inches tall, dark haired, and wearing a pretty, high-necked print dress.

'One and the same.'

'I'm Gail Jennings, a friend of Julia's. She's got stuck in the country, and has asked me to turn up here and make her apologies to you. It's all rather embarrassing. I hope you don't mind.'

Secretly James did mind, as he had been looking forward to a tumble with Julia that night, and did not fancy the prospect of dining with a stranger, picking up the bill for two, and spending the night on his own. He decided, however, to make the best of it.

'Of course not,' he said. 'Her loss is my gain. What would you like to drink?'

'I've already got one, thank you. I've been sitting over there in the corner for the last twenty minutes as I wasn't certain you were the right man. You see, Julia said you were tall, and very good looking.' The girl stopped and blushed. She had not intended this gaffe.

James managed a sickly grin, at the same time sliding off his bar stool and stretching himself to his full five foot nine inches.

'That is, you're not quite how I imagined you'd be,' she added hastily.

James picked up his drink and followed her to her table. Her friendly attitude and relaxed manner meant that conversation came easily.

'Why has Julia never mentioned you before? It's a disgrace keeping someone so pretty hidden from me.'

'Possibly because I've been away for the last two years working in Hong Kong.'

'Was that fun?'

'Fantastic! My elder brother is working out there as an assistant to one of the English racehorse trainers, so I had a ready-made social life.'

'Does that mean you like horse racing?'

'I do now. You can't stay there and not catch the bug. The Chinese are mad on it, particularly the gambling. Aren't you something to do with racing over here? Julia told me you were a good writer but a terrible tipster, and I was to ignore anything you told me to back!'

36

'Charming! To think of all the winners I've given that girl! Yes, I work on a racing newspaper, the *Sportsman*, writing articles and giving punters the names of endless certainties.'

'Do you have any special knowledge about horses? My brother used to spend his whole time studying past performances, the state of the going, the weights, and making knowing comments about this trainer and that jockey, but he still never seemed to back a winner. Can you even ride?'

'I try. I'm what might be called an enthusiastic amateur.'

'Have you ever ridden a winner?'

'Quite a few at point to points, and five under rules, over the jumps.'

'Very impressive! What's been your biggest win to date?'

'Last year at the Cheltenham Festival. I rode the winner of the big amateurs' race, although everyone said afterwards it was the horse that did it, and yours truly only had to hang on.'

'What about the Grand National? Have you ever ridden in that?'

'Not yet, but I'm hoping to this year. The owner of our paper is proposing to offer his beloved horse, aptly called The Sportsman, as a prize in a readers' competition, and part of the small print says I'm to be the jockey.'

'Isn't that dangerous?'

'Who for? Me or the new owner? It can be, of course, but the horse is a marvellous jumper and has a very good trainer, a chap called Archie Duncan at Lambourn. Anyway, that's enough about me. What are your plans now you've returned to the big city?'

'I've just moved into a flat with some girlfriends in Pimlico, and this afternoon I was offered a job as an assistant to a literary agent.'

'Excellent! Don't they spend all day having large lunches, drinking vast amounts of alcohol, and charging it all up to expenses?'

'I think you're confusing them with journalists! From what I've been told, my job is going to involve – eventually, that is, when I've some experience – meeting budding authors, reading manuscripts and seducing publishers with my charms.'

'I hope you leave it there! It all sounds fairly agreeable. How about celebrating over dinner?'

'Are you sure? I mean, I'm here under false pretences!'

'Don't be ridiculous! It'll be my pleasure. Have you any preferences?'

'I'll pretty well eat anything. Though I'd prefer a break from Chinese.'

Thank God, thought James, remembering the last time he'd made a fool of himself with the chopsticks. 'How about Italian, then? I know a very friendly one not far from my flat in Fulham, or rather Chelsea, as the estate agents like to say. What's more, if we're lucky, we won't have to listen to any Italian waiters singing happy birthday to some embarrassed diner.'

Gail laughed. 'Or sit next to a couple discussing house prices in Parson's Green!'

James managed a smile. *He* was used to cracking the jokes.

James was made as welcome at Angelo's as a bookmaker's cheque. Angelo himself loved the occasional wager, and from his enthusiastic greeting it seemed that James had tipped him a winner on his last visit. After dinner sambuccas were to be on the house!

The pair were ushered to a candle-lit corner table, as Angelo gave James a knowing wink. James' Italian –

which he sometimes tried on the proprietor – did not extend to 'we're just good friends'. He doubted whether Italians knew of such a relationship anyway. Angelo ran through a list of special dishes, but as James remarked to Gail, the choice was basically pasta, or pasta, followed by chicken or veal in a number of different disguises.

After they had ordered, Gail asked him if he had always wanted to be a journalist.

'Not at all. All I ever thought about was horses, and as soon as I finished school and university I took a job as an assistant to a trainer in Newmarket.'

'Why did you give it up then?'

'No option, I'm afraid. My father was a vicar and when he died suddenly three years ago we found that while spiritually very rich, he was materially very overdrawn. So someone had to earn enough to pay my sister's school fees, and yours truly took up the pen as a result. I can't complain. I'm fairly well-paid and spend my life hanging around race tracks.'

'Doesn't that ever get boring?'

'Boring? Why, only today I overheard a murder being committed!'

'You what?' Gail's expression turned to one of genuine horror.

'And what's more, I discovered the body!'

'I don't believe you! Go on, tell me the details.'

'It's true! I had arranged to meet a stable lad, who sells me information, at Newbury races, in a field where they park the boxes. Only I overslept on the race train and by the time I got there he'd gone. Just as I was leaving, I heard what sounded like a scuffle followed by an agonising groan.' James went on to recount the drama of discovering the dead body.

Gail listened in amazement. 'How ghastly! Do the police know who he was?'

'I saved them the trouble. It was the Senior Steward of the Jockey Club. Old Sir Denby Croft.'

'The poor man. Do they know who did it?'

James looked at her across the dinner table. 'Would it worry you to know that you are dining with a murder suspect?'

Gail smiled. 'It depends on whether he's innocent or not.'

'I'm glad to say that I am, although the police don't seem that eager to accept my protestations. I'm not helped by that idiot of a stable lad – his name's Paddy. He even denied knowing me when they questioned him!'

'Why would he do that?'

'A touch of the MI5s. He'll change his mind after I've had a word with him tomorrow. The final irony was that Croft's horse won the big race, although it was too late to give his owner any pleasure.'

'I suppose your sensational discovery will be the headline in tomorrow's *Sportsman*?'

'I certainly hope so. It's not every year I get to write the lead story. In fact, the last one I wrote two years ago was such a disaster, they keep me away from so-called news stories.'

'Why, what was that about? Not another murder, I hope?'

'Nothing so trivial. I wrote an exposé of one Morton Marsh, who's a pretty famous trainer, accusing him of doping the occasional horse to make them run faster. Trouble is, he's now suing the *Sportsman* and myself for defamation of character, and my source has done a runner, a bunk.'

'When's the case coming to court?'

'Too soon. It's due to be heard in a couple of months, some time after Christmas. But if nothing turns up soon, I expect the lawyers will tell us to settle and pay damages. And you know whose head will be on the chopping block then.'

'They wouldn't actually sack you for that, would they?'

'They might. It would help if I could come up with something on who killed Sir Denby. Do you fancy a bit of private sleuthing?'

'You mean, "Brunette saves journalist from murder rap"? I'll think about it. I suppose if you lost your job, you'd make your living off betting?'

'Not with my record. In fact, I need to keep my job to win the biggest bet I've ever had.'

'What's that?'

'On myself to win the Naps Competition. The *Sporting Life* compiles a table of the daily naps nominated by a number of racing journalists and the winner at the end of the season is the tipster whose daily nap shows the biggest profit to a pound stake.'

'What's the prize?'

'About £1000, or something, but more important, I've had a thousand pounds to win £16,000 on myself with my bookie. If I win, I'm rich, and all my debts are paid.'

'And if you lose?'

James pulled a face and changed the subject.

They chatted merrily throughout the rest of dinner and even managed to squeeze an extra free sambucca out of Angelo. By 12.30, James was still feeling full of energy.

'Do you fancy dancing?' he asked Gail.

'Isn't it a bit late?'

'Come on, we're only young once; it's not every day I discover a dead body!'

'All right then. Where shall we go? Are you a member of any clubs?'

'No, but a friend of mine is a member of Bunter's,

41

and if I give his name, we'll probably be able to slip in.'

James found dancing to soul music very difficult. He could just about locate the beat, but his brain was quite incapable of translating it to his feet. He moved self-consciously and woodenly around the floor, while Gail laughed and swayed effortlessly in front of him. Occasionally he swung her round, partly to reflect his enthusiasm, mostly as an excuse for some kind of physical contact.

He was greatly relieved when the slow music began, and he could at last hold Gail in his arms. Having steadfastly refused dance lessons at school, his main concern, as he shuffled back and forth, was not to stand on her toes. He decided to hold her tightly against his body to test her reaction. She didn't push him away. In fact, she smiled as he kissed her playfully on the cheek.

At 2.15 a.m., he suggested that perhaps they ought to leave. As they sat in his car, he ventured that she might just like a coffee to end the evening. Gail looked him straight in the eye, and almost disconcertingly answered, 'Yes, that would be nice.'

Well over the limit, James drove carefully back to Redcliffe Gardens, and led Gail up to the third floor flat he called home.

Chapter 4

James woke up alone the next morning. Struggling out of bed, the *Sportsman*'s young tipster went and collected that morning's edition of his newspaper from its resting place on the hall carpet. He then headed for the kitchen and a large cup of coffee to soothe his hangover. Trust his luck, he reflected, to have teamed up with one of the few girls left in London who, when they said they would come back for a cup of coffee, meant just that. Gail had stayed for an hour before telephoning for a taxi to take her home. She had declined James' offer of a lift on the evidence of his driving from the night club. One curb could be regarded as an accident but three were less readily explained. At least she had kissed him goodnight and agreed to go with him to Newbury to watch the

Hennessy and more importantly to find Paddy Develera and persuade him to drop his role as an MI5 operative and tell the police how he had arranged to meet James.

The headline 'Man on the Run to Finish Alone' meant that Denby's death had been relegated to the second lead. Still, the story had made the front page: 'Drama at Newbury Races' by James Thackeray. He was not so keen on the description that followed: 'Our Man on the Spot'. The way things were looking, 'in a spot' would have been more appropriate. That apart, Denis the chief sub-editor had hardly altered a word, leaving in all the gory details of how the murdered man was discovered.

The phone rang. It was James's mother. Ever since his father's death she'd looked to James for both financial and moral support and though at times it could be a little oppressive he loved her dearly.

'Are you all right?' she asked anxiously.

'What do you mean?'

'I've just heard on the news about this terrible murder. You're not in trouble, are you, James?'

'Of course not. I just discovered the body.'

'Are you sure that's all?'

'Isn't that enough?'

'It's too much as far as I'm concerned. You always were careless. It's just that the man on the radio said that a young journalist called James Thackeray has been helping police with their enquiries, and in my experience that's a rather costly gesture.'

'Don't believe everything you hear on the news. As you see, mother, I'm here to answer your call and nobody's suggested, or at least not yet, that they're about to lock me up.'

'You just watch out. I've lost a husband and I've no intention of losing my son.'

'Hear, hear. I'll keep in touch, don't worry.'

James put down the receiver and went to have a shave. It was clearly more important than ever that he should find Paddy Develera.

He had arranged to pick up Gail early from her flat, as he wanted to avoid the queue of Renault 5s laden with brown Trilbies and Hermes scarves which traditionally blocked all roads leading to Newbury in the National Hunt season. Furthermore he was reluctant to ask too much of the ageing Morris Traveller which his father had once used to tour his parish. Gail seemed very pleased to see him and looked, he thought, really quite pretty with her dark hair tied behind her neck in a yellow ribbon, an unintentional tribute to the late Senior Steward. They arrived at the racecourse in good time and the atmosphere in the press room perceptibly brightened when James entered with Gail in tow. There was a good deal of banter and wisecracking. A man from the *Echo*, a noted wag, drew her aside and explained in apparent seriousness that James's naps were going so badly that he would have stooped to anything to get Paradise Lost withdrawn from the big race. James smirked. It wasn't every day of the week that one got mixed up in a murder inquiry *and* was able to show off a pretty girl.

After the first two races the couple made their way to the parade ring where the lads were leading round the runners for the Hennessey, and managed to fight their way through the crowd to a place on the rails. James soon spotted Paddy walking Jack the Lad round. Monty Spry's charge looked very much on his toes and carried his head proudly, which was more than could be said of Paddy, who stared at the ground ahead of him as if he was expecting at any moment to find a ten pound note.

They waited until after the horses had paraded in front of the packed stands and cantered off to the start.

Then James grabbed Paddy as he set off for his usual haunt in the betting shop. The Irishman seemed reluctant to talk to him..

'Why the hell did you tell the police that you didn't know me? You've got me in a right mess.'

'How did I know what they wanted? Sure as anything they would have reported me to the guv'nor and I'd be out of a job.'

'Will you tell them now?' interrupted Gail.

'And who are you?'

· 'She's with me,' James butted in.

'No,' said Paddy, shaking his head. 'I don't think I can. You see, I can't have the police asking too many questions about me past, now.'

'You're not wanted, are you?'

'No, no, nothing like that. Just a bit of confusion over the contents of a petty-cash box at the firm where I worked in Dublin. Anyways I can't be helping the police very much. I only saw them for a couple of seconds before I left.'

'Who were they?'

'How should I know?' replied Paddy somewhat evasively. 'Now look here, Mr James, do me a favour and leave me out of this.'

James looked forlorn and was extremely surprised when Gail started to speak. 'In that case, Paddy, you leave us no option but to tell your governor that you've been selling information about horses in his yard. I don't think he'll be too pleased about that, somehow.'

Paddy's face fell even further. 'You wouldn't be doing that, would you?'

'We would,' replied Gail and James in unison.

Paddy reflected. 'Okay, you win. I'll tell them that we arranged to meet but that when you didn't show I pissed off.'

'Good. And if I were you I'd also tell them about

those people you saw.'

'What people?' said Paddy, looking James straight in the eye and feigning dumb innocence.

Jack the Lad duly won the The Hennessey from Man on the Run, and at the end of the day's racing James and Gail found Paddy celebrating his victory in the bar beside the paddock. The eight empty Guinness bottles lined up on the counter beside him were an ominous indication as to his condition. He seemed to have forgotten completely about the proposed visit to the police and instead insisted on repeatedly drinking Gail's health and asking what a pretty girl like her was doing with a mean sod like James. Eventually they had no option but to grab his arms, frogmarch him to the car and then drive to Newbury.

The police sergeant at the desk was clearly unimpressed by the sight of a drunken Irishman, supported, with some difficulty, on either side, and shook his head when James asked if they could see Inspector Hardcastle.

'I'm afraid he's busy, sir. Looking at your friend here, I suggest you take him home.'

Paddy agreed with this suggestion and started to make a bolt for the door but James just beat him to it and hauled him back. 'Sorry, Sergeant, but it is urgent. I have some information in the Croft case and I would be grateful if you could just tell the inspector that James Thackeray is here with Paddy Develera and would appreciate five minutes of his time.'

The sergeant reluctantly went away and on his return told them that the inspector would see them at once. They were ushered into a large room with a row of filing cabinets lined up against one wall. Behind the desk sat the inspector and opposite him, with his back to the door, a short plump man in an ill-fitting dark blue suit. Chief Superintendent Pale was introduced to James and shook him firmly by the hand. He smiled benignly at Gail whom James introduced along with Paddy.

'I'm sorry to burst in upon you, Inspector and Superintendent, but Mr Develera has, I think, something to say to you.' James gave Paddy a prod. The Irishman swayed on his feet and looked down towards the floor. His yellow complexion was an ominous omen.

'Really?' said Inspector Hardcastle. 'Yesterday Mr Develera told us that he'd never met you. Changed his mind, has he? Or was it a temporary loss of memory? A touch of the St Peter's?'

Paddy looked up rather sheepishly. 'I think I must have misheard you yesterday, sir. I know this fellow well and he and I had arranged to do a little business, but he failed to show.'

'Is that now all right?' asked James. 'Am I in the clear?'

'Yes, you're in the clear. As I was just telling Chief Superintendent Pale, his trip from London has been a waste of time. We already know who murdered Sir Denby Croft.'

'Who?' asked Gail, unable to contain her excitement.

'A man we arrested this morning at Malton. A certain George Weatherby. Looks like your first instinct was right, Mr Thackeray.'

Chapter 5

Three weeks later George Weatherby was committed for trial at Reading Crown Court for the murder of Sir Denby Croft. Although public interest in the affair had already begun to wane, there was a fairly large press attendance for the short committal proceedings at Newbury Magistrates' Court.

James was due to go to Worcester races but could not resist stopping at Newbury en route. He was still very troubled by the circumstances of Sir Denby's death and somehow felt that Weatherby was too obvious a culprit.

'Why choose your own horsebox in which to murder a man?' he had asked Gail over dinner at her flat the night before.

She had thought for a moment before answering.

'It's not such a silly place. If you hadn't come along at the wrong time, Weatherby would have got away with it. He could have driven away from the course with old Denby in the back and disposed of his body at his leisure. What a dreadful thought!'

'I suppose you're right. And handing over a horse to another trainer gave him the perfect excuse for being at the course. Some revenge!'

'That's Weatherby's problem now, and not yours. You should be grateful that the police have found a suitable murderer and are no longer interested in you. Have some more wine and stop moping.'

James had never met Weatherby but he'd seen him often enough on the racecourse. In the dock he looked a different man. Gone were the arrogant air and fiery red cheeks and in their place a worried frown and pallid complexion. The large bags under his eyes suggested that he had not slept much since his arrest.

Once the court clerk had read out the charge, the committal procedure was over in seconds. Nobody mentioned bail, but Weatherby's solicitor, a chap of about James's age in a dark pinstriped suit, made a short statement to the Bench.

'Through me, my client wishes to make it clear that he vehemently denies this charge. These proceedings will be strenuously defended at trial and I appeal for any witness who saw my client between 12.30 and 1.30 on the day of the murder to come forward.'

The unmoved expressions on the faces of the magistrates made James feel that they had heard this kind of speech before. Accompanied by two prison officers Weatherby was led away from the dock, and, James supposed, back to prison. He decided to talk to Weatherby's solicitor.

'Excuse me, you're acting for Mr Weatherby, aren't you?'

'I hoped that was obvious from my speech. If you're from the press there's nothing more I can say to you.'

'I'm a journalist but that's not why I'm here. I'm James Thackeray, the man who discovered the body.'

'Yes, I've heard of you. I've got your statement to the police somewhere. It's a bit of a shame you didn't catch the murderer in the act. Then my client wouldn't be in this mess.'

'Do you think he's innocent, then?'

'That's not for me to decide. It's for the police to prove he's guilty, but I'm afraid they seem pretty confident.'

'Oh. I probably shouldn't say this but the whole thing seems too easy, too obvious.'

'I agree with you. I've only met Weatherby a couple of times and he doesn't strike me as the killing type. My firm's only doing the job as his usual solicitor up north is out of his depth. Murder defences are a far cry from pleas in front of the beaks at Malton for driving without due care.'

James looked up across the court and could see Inspector Hardcastle glaring at him. 'If I can be of any assistance I'd be delighted.'

'Thanks for the offer. But unless you can find someone to back up his alibi I don't see what you can do.'

'You could at least tell me what the case against him consists of. The racing world is full of wild rumours. One so-called informed source is claiming that as Croft lay dying, he wrote Weatherby's name in the horse dung on the floor!'

'Nothing so melodramatic! Look, I've got an hour before my train back to London. Let's go and have a cup of coffee and I'll tell you what the police say happened, but promise to keep it to yourself.'

'It's a promise.'

* * *

51

Fergus Pollock, as the solicitor was called, spoke rapidly and in hushed tones. He told James how the police had discovered a message in the top pocket of Sir Denby's suit which had obviously been compiled from newspaper cuttings and which accused him of cheating. It was the police theory that Weatherby had sent him the note as the first step in a plan to murder him.

'Weatherby plainly had a motive, as Croft had in effect destroyed his career. The police are certain that had you not stumbled along at just the wrong time he would have driven the box away and disposed of the body. Bringing a horse down to transfer it to another trainer gave him a concrete explanation for being at the racecourse.'

'What does he say he was doing between 12.30 and 1.30?'

'As you probably know, he didn't, or rather couldn't, have a runner at the meeting. He claims that a man called Hoskins telephoned him the night before, and arranged to meet him at 12.45 at the racecourse to discuss a possible job as a racing advisor. Needless to say, this Hoskins fellow never turned up, and Weatherby waited at their agreed rendezvous for over an hour.'

'But didn't he meet or see anyone he knew?'

'Well, he says not. He deliberately kept away from the race crowd. A disgraced trainer is about as popular as a gelding standing at stud, if you think about it. And an innocent person doesn't walk around looking for potential alibi witnesses.'

James could see the logic of that. 'I've got to go to Worcester, but can I have your number in case I think of anything?'

'Certainly,' said Fergus. 'Here's my card. I'm normally in court during the day, but don't hesitate to phone and leave a message if anything comes up.'

Chapter 6

James decided to leave Worcester after the fifth race. He wanted to have a talk with Paddy and did not want to bump into Monty Spry at his yard when he did so. Since the trainer had a runner in the last race he had every chance of seeing the Irishman, who was not at the races that day, and being on the road back to London before his governor returned.

He drove to Compton, parked his Morris fifty yards down the road from the stable entrance, and walked into the well-lit yard. It was a bustle of activity. The lads were giving the horses their evening feed, and nobody took much notice of James as he stood on the cobbled courtyard which was surrounded by boxes full of expensive animals. In his tweed coat and dark flannel suit he looked like an owner who had turned up unannounced, and Jamed devoutly hoped that the lads would take him for such. He felt apprehensive. He had successfully timed his visit to avoid Monty, but was even keener not to come across Gordon, Monty's head lad. The latter had been in racing for years, having worked for Monty's late father. Gordon was regarded as one of the old school, whatever that meant, and had a notorious aversion to amateur jockeys. On the one occasion when James had, at the owner's insistence, ridden a horse from the yard, Gordon had gone out of his way to show his displeasure. The fact that it had been a winner had only added to his ill-humour. He was feared among the stable staff for his strict discipline and was alleged to make Wackford Squeers look like Mother Teresa.

James walked up to a young lad carrying a bucket of water to one of the boxes. 'I'm looking for Paddy Develera. Is he around?'

The lad hesitated. 'Paddy? I haven't seen him ... '

Before he could finish, Gordon's unmistakable bald head appeared from within the half-open box. 'And who wants to know? Oh, it's you, is it, *Mr* Thackeray?'

James winced at the sarcastic emphasis on the word mister. 'Yes. Hello, Gordon. I'm sorry to barge in here unannounced, but I wanted to have a short chat with Paddy.'

'What about?' Gordon's tone was scarcely conciliatory.

'Good question. The *Sportsman* want to do a series of articles about a day in the life of a hard-working stable lad and someone suggested your Paddy.'

Gordon looked at him in disbelief. 'I think someone's been pulling your leg. Anyway, Paddy hasn't been here for the last two days and if he doesn't pitch up at first lot tomorrow you'll be writing a piece about a day in the life of an unemployed stable lad.'

'Has anyone checked up to see if he's all right?'

'Mr Thackeray, I run a racing stable, not a citizens advice bureau.'

'All right, all right, I get the message. At least you could tell me where he lives.'

'In lodgings somewhere near East Hendred.'

The young lad now reappeared. 'I think it's with Mrs Rivers,' he said. 'They'll be able to tell you at any of the pubs in the village.'

James returned to his car. It refused to start. He paled at the prospect of asking Gordon for a push, and tried again. Eventually the engine spluttered grudgingly into life.

It was raining as James walked through the door of The Old Sickle. Ordering a pint, he sat at the bar and waited for an opportunity to talk to the landlord. Business was quiet and he did not have to wait long.

'I suppose you get a fair number of racing people in here?'

'Quite a lot. Enjoy their drink, too, some of 'em.'

'And why not? There's a lad used to look after one of a friend of mine's horses who I think lives down this way now. Could be one of your regulars, an Irish fellow.'

'We get a lot of 'em in 'ere. Racing mad, they are.'

'This one's about five feet four and would be in his late thirties. He always wears a filthy green anorak. Paddy is his name.'

'You mean Paddy Develera? The one who lodges with Mrs Rivers up the road?'

'Could be him.' James tried not to sound too enthusiastic.

'Comes from Dublin and likes to act very secretive when he discusses his boss's horses?'

'Yes, that sounds just like him,' James replied.

'He's always coming in here. Loves his beer and a singsong of a Saturday night. In fact, I had to ban him for a couple of weeks from last Wednesday.'

'Why was that?'

'He's been impossible lately. Seems to be full of money since his horse won the Hennessy. Been getting extremely drunk, upsetting my other regulars.' The landlord went on drying glasses. 'Got to think of all the customers in this game. No one man's bigger than a pub, that's what I say.'

James nodded in agreement. 'You couldn't tell me where Mrs Rivers' house is, could you? Sounds like he's rich enough to buy me a drink.'

'No trouble. Go out the village as if you're going back to Wantage and you'll come across a row of terraced houses on your left. It's the third or fourth in the middle. You can't miss it. It's painted pink on the outside.'

'Thanks. I'll look him up.'

'Doubt if you'll find him home as early as this. He doesn't get away from work until about seven and then it's about a forty-minute bike ride.'

'Oh, well, no harm in trying. Thanks for your help. Here, have one on me.' James slipped a pound coin across the counter.

A fat jolly woman opened the door of the pink house, and with a friendly smile asked James what he wanted. It was a far cry from the greeting a stranger would receive in the city. Mrs Rivers must have been in her late sixties and was wearing an apron with the words 'Buy British' across the front.

James came straight to the point. 'I'm sorry to disturb you, but I'm here about Mr Develera who I understand lodges with you.'

'Yes, he's one of my lodgers. Do come in. It's far too cold to stand talking on the doorstep.'

James was shown into a brightly furnished lounge where a log fire was roaring away and made to sit down on a sofa covered in a loud floral patterned material.

'I'm just cooking supper, so forgive my apron. Paddy's all right, isn't he?'

The question took James by surprise. 'What do you mean? Isn't he staying here?'

'Yes, but he hasn't been home for a couple of days and I was beginning to get a bit worried. I thought you might be from the stables. Every now and again he doesn't come back from the pub but he's always turned up the following night vowing never to touch another drop.'

James attempted to be reassuring. 'I'm sure he'll turn up tonight. Did he perhaps tell you where he was going the other evening?'

'No, but I think he was going to meet a friend. He wasn't one for telling me his plans and I'm not one for asking. My late husband always said a man's private life is just that and that's always been my way of thinking towards my lodgers.'

'Very understanding of you, Mrs Rivers.'

She was now in full flight. 'There's one thing, though,' she continued. 'Three nights ago — that's just before he, er, went away — a man phoned asking for him. I answered, as I usually do.'

'Did he give a name?'

'No, he was a bit short with me. He just asked to speak to Paddy so I went and fetched him and he took the call.'

'Did he say anything about it afterwards?'

'Yes. He quite surprised me. He said something about how jockeys as well as journalists were now wanting to pick his brains and with the information he had he was

57

soon going to be very rich. Then he said it was heaven-sent, and I asked him why, and he laughed. He said' – Mrs Rivers now paused briefly for effect – 'he said it was heaven-sent because the jockey's name was Angell. Funny that, wasn't it?'

James nodded. He did not want to upset Mrs Rivers and in any event he had no real reason to feel worried. Willie Angell was one of the most unscrupulous jockeys in racing and James had on more than one occasion written about his riding performances in unflattering terms. Even Morton Marsh had been forced to sack him as his stable jockey. He was notorious for dirty tricks and in particular for pulling horses. A racecourse wit had once nicknamed him 'The Ancient Mariner' because 'he stoppeth one of three', and the name had stuck, although not many of the racing establishment, including Willie himself, had grasped the literary reference. However, running horses to suit the bookies and forcing rivals onto the rails were not proof of a murderous predisposition outside the race-track. Or were they? Saying good-bye to a still voluble Mrs Rivers, James walked thoughtfully towards his car.

Chapter 7

James did not go into the *Sportsman*'s offices until the following morning, having telephoned his copy and selections for that day's events from the racecourse at Worcester. When he arrived at his desk he found a note from the editor's secretary. He was to go and see Carlton as soon as he got in.

The great man finished dictating a letter and asked James to sit down on the leather sofa which ran along one whole side of the room. The walls were decorated with photographs of the winners of famous races and there was an oil painting of Carlton himself, commissioned by his staff to celebrate twenty-five years as editor.

'James, I think it's time you and I had a serious chat. We've been very pleased with your work since you joined us and I think it's fair to say we've treated you well in return, and given you plenty of time off to ride as an amateur.'

James began to feel uneasy. He had never been sacked before and he wondered if this was the prelude to the big heave-ho.

Carlton continued, his voice as friendly as ever. 'However, certain problems are looming up and I'm anxious we should sort them out now.'

James could merely nod.

'Firstly I had a call last night from an Inspector Hardcastle about the Denby Croft case. Apparently he saw you yesterday at the committal hearing and you went off and had coffee with the defence lawyer. The inspector quite rightly pointed out that you will almost certainly be called as a witness for the prosecution, and shouldn't be getting involved with the other side. From my point of view, which is also the paper's, you're paid to be a racing journalist. If you want to be a crime reporter, which God forbid, you'll have to take your considerable talents elsewhere.

'Next, and more important, is that article you wrote about Morton Marsh doping his horses. I've had a long, detailed and no doubt extremely expensive letter from our solicitors saying that the libel action is going to be heard in the second week of January and our case is in a shambles. That stable lad ... what's his name?'

'Milford.'

'Yes, Milford, who gave you all the information for the article, is refusing to co-operate and we've had no luck with the vet – Jackson, wasn't it? – who did the dirty work, either. In short things are looking distinctly gloomy. We're going to see leading counsel in his chambers this afternoon and I want you to be there. I don't want to give in on this one and I only hope that our beloved proprietor will back me.

'And that leads to my final point. It was an extremely generous gesture on the part of our proprietor to let us offer a horse as a prize to our readers. Some would say it was an act of rank madness for him to let you ride The Sportsman in the National. Still I couldn't dissuade him from it.' James smiled for the first time. The idea had been Carlton's as both men very well knew. 'I talked to our trainer this morning on the phone. Duncan says the horse is in excellent shape and thinks he's in with a real chance if the handicapper treats him fairly.'

Carlton paused and looked across at James.

'What's your weight at the moment?'

James sat up straight and tightened his stomach muscles. 'Eleven stone ten, but I'm about to start serious training.'

'You'd better, because Duncan reckons that you'll get ten twelve in the National and if you're as much as a pound overweight you needn't come in the following Monday. Now go away and find some winners. You're doing bloody awfully in the Naps table. I can't see why we pay all that money for that chap in Spry's yard when you stand by and allow us to tip something else in the Hennessy.'

James almost told him about Paddy but decided against it. Instead, he returned to his desk, somewhat shaken. Gail was busy when he tried to telephone her, 'in conference' with an author about the publicity for his new book. Disconsolately he got down to the weary business of repairing his tattered reputation as a tipster.

Eric Soper, doyen of greyhound journalists, came over to talk. He had worked as the paper's greyhound tipster and crime correspondent for as long as anyone could remember, and claimed to have been present as a young man at all of Mick the Miller's victories. Since Eric was now forty-five and Mick the Miller had won all his races in 1930, James took some of his yarns with a pinch of salt. Perhaps he had been a hare in his previous life. When James had arrived to work on the *Sportsman* three years earlier Eric had befriended him, and together they had enjoyed many evenings at Eric's house with his wife Jane and their two young daughters.

James told Eric about the editor's lecture and his own anxieties about Paddy. Eric listened patiently, and then said, 'I think Carlton's right. The case against Weatherby may look a bit too simple but that doesn't mean that Paddy knows something of importance. He's probably lying in a ditch somewhere, recovering from a two-day bender. He'll turn up, you take my word. The trouble with you young men is you're too eager for adventure. I would concentrate on that new girl of yours, you've been talking so much about. Sounds a much better way of using up your excess energy – and losing some of that weight.'

James laughed. He had no desire to be a hero and reflected that perhaps he ought to take the advice of others and mind his own business. His job plainly depended on it.

The meeting with the lawyers took place in counsel's chambers in the Temple. Sir Crichton Blade was charming, yet firm. He made it plain that in the absence of the testimony of the stable lad, Milford, the paper's case was hopeless. It was resolved to serve a subpoena on him to ensure his attendance at the trial. The only problem, as Mr Gilbert Twine, the paper's shy, dry and wily solicitor, crisply remarked, was finding him in order to serve it.

James left the conference feeling distinctly low. As he walked past the Middle Temple church, he thought of his father. The old boy, in spite of his cloth, had been an avid racing fan, and had even encouraged James' interest in betting. Indeed, his own favourite wager was an across-the-card patent – The Holy Trinity as he irreverently called it. James sadly missed his support and advice now. He only hoped that a couple of weeks at home with his mother and sister over Christmas and the New Year would allow him to gain a proper sense of perspective.

As it happened, he saw far more of Gail than his family over the festive season. She refused to let him wander round with a long face and together they went to party after party. James was just feeling in need of another holiday to recover when he was told that the case of Marsh versus the *Sportsman* and Thackeray was listed to be heard on the second Monday in January.

Chapter 8

The Honourable Mr Justice Bindworth stormed into Court Number 14 and scowled. He looked like a winning owner whose jockey had forgotten to weigh in. James could only hope that all Her Majesty's judges looked like this on a Monday morning. In fact, as far as this pillar of the judiciary was concerned, today was exceptional. Outside the Royal Courts of Justice, and usually in them as well, Sir Reggie Bindworth was one of the most genial of fellows. It was just unfortunate that over breakfast, on this particular Monday morning, his wife Georgina had dropped a bombshell. Her elder sister Agnes was coming to stay for a couple of weeks to recuperate from an operation – not, alas, on her vocal chords. That was bad enough. But Georgina had also insisted that he cancel his proposed weekend's golf, which was unforgiveable.

James looked around him. It was his first appearance in court in any capacity. Morton Marsh had retained the services of Sir Desmond Stanley, and that eminent QC was now seated nearest the empty jury box, nervously playing with the red ribbon which adorns every barrister's brief to appear in court. Well over six foot tall, with a full head of hair, a long cadaverous face with high cheek bones, he was easily the most imposing figure in the courtroom, and at 56 years of age was widely regarded by both bench and bar, but not by his mistress, as being at the height of his powers. The scale of his fees bore testimony to his fame and prowess. It was rumoured that he would not appear in any trial for a fee of under £10,000 with a daily refresher of £750. Clearly Marsh was prepared to spare no expense to win this action.

On Sir Desmond's right, casually leaning his head against the back of the pew, sat Sir Crichton Blade. For him the end of a glorious career was drawing near. Indeed it had recently been suggested in the press that this might be his last case. How sad, thought James, that it seemed destined to end in a crushing defeat. Dressed like Sir Desmond in a silk gown, the privilege and hallmark of Queen's Counsel, Sir Crichton Blade was a mere five foot six inches, but his small frame belied a force of advocacy and a power of persuasion that could at times be positively breathtaking. No one who had witnessed it would ever forget his majestic yet clinical closing speech for the defence in the Bournemouth Wheelchair Case — and there had been many similar triumphs. It was said that he had turned down the offer of a judgeship on no fewer than three occasions. For him, the cut and thrust of life was at the bar, not up there on the bench in the place occupied so comfortably by Sir Reggie.

James's eyes moved on. They rested only a moment on the row of junior counsel, sitting behind their leaders, rustling their papers and notes, and generally trying to look useful and important, and settled on Morton Marsh. His antagonist looked depressingly confident, James thought. Dapper and erect, his moustache freshly clipped, he smiled for a moment as he caught his wife's eye. His bland self-assurance contrasted in every respect with the feelings, if not the outward appearance, of James and his editor. Carlton Williams had never shrunk from legal battles in the past, but James knew he had gone out on a limb in fighting this case and was now extremely apprehensive. Most of all, he was worried, as was James himself, by the absence of their two key witnesses, Jackson the vet and Milford the stable lad. James took one final, despairing glance round. Not a sign of either of them, of course.

Within a few minutes the twelve jurors had been selected – five men and seven women, to James's chagrin. He had hoped at least for a dominance of males, some of whom could be expected to be sympathetic punters. He did not feel encouraged as the jury took the oath and settled into their seats. Sir Reggie, however, seemed contented enough with the arrangements. He surveyed his court, gave a slight nod of his head, barked a curt 'Yes, Sir Desmond', and they were ready to start.

With a leisurely movement, Sir Desmond Stanley rose to his feet, turned to the jury, and without glancing at the notes on the lectern in front of him, started to speak. 'May it please your lordship, ladies and gentlemen of the jury, in this action for libel, for damage to reputation, I appear on behalf of the plaintiff, with my learned junior, Mr Culpepper, whilst my learned friend, Sir Crichton Blade, appears, with Mr

Twain, for the defendants, publishers of the *Sportsman* newspaper, and Mr James Thackeray, a journalist. The plaintiff in this action, Mr Morton Marsh, is a well-known racehorse trainer, a man who has the distinction of having trained the winners of over four hundred races, including the winner of the Gold Cup, regarded as the blue riband of National Hunt racing. He numbers among his owners such reputable members of society as the Duke of Metton, and numerous other respectable devotees of what is affectionately known as the Sport of Kings.'

James glanced at the jury. They seemed mesmerized already, curse them.

'It would be no exaggeration,' Sir Desmond's sonorous voice went on, 'to say that the plaintiff has deservedly risen to the top of his profession. Indeed, at the time when the article which is the subject of these proceedings was published, he had over fifty horses in training in his yard, and had already won in that season alone over £100,000 in prize money. But as you will hear, the pride and joy he took in his work was suddenly and viciously destroyed overnight, when the *Sportsman*, the prominent racing paper, read by the very people with and among whom he spent his life, published an article entitled "One man's way to beat the handicapper". This article, which we shall shortly read together, was written by Mr James Thackeray, the second defendant. I don't think I do him an injustice when I say that Mr Thackeray is a young and inexperienced journalist – but that is a subject we will return to later in this trial. (Must we? thought James). Regrettably, members of the jury, you will have to contrast the limitations of that experience with the unlimited innuendo with which Mr Thackeray was prepared to attack the character and integrity of my client. Let us now read that article together ... '

With a dramtic flourish, Sir Desmond handed down to the usher copies of the article to give to the jury. They were eagerly accepted.

Politely but firmly, Sir Desmond asked them to wait before reading the contents, as it would be a much easier task done together, he said. He then proceeded in his slow deep voice to read the article aloud. James closed his eyes. He would also like to have been able to close his ears, as line by line Sir Desmond proceeded to dissect his rather flat prose. There was something masterful about the way in which counsel extracted so much offensive meaning from the simple concluding statement, that Mr Marsh's conduct ought now to be the subject of an investigation by the Jockey Club. He intoned those last words as if they amounted to the announcement of a death sentence.

James opened his eyes and looked at the jury. They were lapping it up. One woman in particular, in the front row, in a rather prim brown suit with a contrastingly loud purple scarf around her neck, was giving him a filthy look. She reminded James of his Aunt Deidre.

Having finished his analysis of the article, Sir Desmond was now pressing on with his peroration. But whereas a more conventional pleader would have pulled out all the stops at this stage, Sir Desmond dropped his voice to an almost confidential pitch, as though he were addressing each juror privately in his drawing room.

'Well, members of the jury, I suspect that you will agree with me that the meaning of that article is clear. It plainly accuses my client of doping horses and thereby achieving a number of undeserved victories. If such allegations were true, then he ought to be, as would no doubt occur, drummed out of racing. I believe the correct phrase is "warned off Newmarket Heath". '

Sir Desmond paused. A male juror in his mid-thirties, wearing a rather dishevelled grey suit and an open-necked shirt, nodded in agreement. James winced. The only punter on the jury, and already on the other side.

'Ladies and gentlemen.' Sir Desmond now switched his histrionic tactics and began to quicken the pace. 'You can well imagine the effect this article has had on my client and the racing fraternity. You will hear from his own lips how he was cut dead by two fellow trainers at Wincanton races on the day of publication, and how he had to reassure his owners that its contents were without foundation. Some tragically believed the old adage that there is no smoke without fire, and chose to take their horses away. Happily, the great majority have stayed loyal. Quite properly, Mr Marsh sought an immediate withdrawal and apology from the *Sportsman*'s publishers. To this day, none has been forthcoming. Worse than that, the newspaper and the journalist have maintained that the central accusation of the article, that of doping, was true. We all wait with baited breath to see whom they will call to back up the particulars pleaded in their defence. It is our guess that the witness box you see over there (Sir Desmond dramatically pointed to it at the other end of the court) will remain as empty as the rhetoric and allegations which fill this article. Soon, members of the jury, I will call Morton Marsh to give his evidence under oath, and at the end of the trial, I will ask you to award him a substantial sum by way of damages, not by way of punishment, but as compensation and vindication of his character.'

James looked around the courtroom, and spotted Gail, standing near the door. She smiled encouragingly and winked at him. With considerable difficulty he managed to smile back.

'I now call Morton Marsh,' said Sir Desmond gravely.

Marsh, smartly dressed in a tweed suit, shining brown brogues and what looked like a regimental tie, walked confidently to the witness box. He took the oath, gave his name and address and, in a clear voice, answered the questions put to him by Sir Desmond. Even his moustache seemed to bristle with self-importance. The court heard of his distinguished training record, of how he never gambled on horses, of how hurt and shocked he had been by the *Sportsman*'s allegations. They had, he said, cast a depressing shadow on an otherwise successful and happy career. His purpose in bringing these proceedings was to clear his name. The judge was visibly impressed. He interrupted on only two occasions, the first time to clarify the gravity of an accusation of doping, and the second, even more tellingly, to ask Marsh about his war record.

'Yes, my lord, I spent five years in the Royal Artillery, seeing active service in North Africa and Italy. I had the additional honour of being mentioned three times in despatches.' And once too often in the *Sportsman*, thought James, as he visualised another nought being added to the damages.

By now it was 12.55, and soon it would be Sir Crichton's turn to cross-examine Marsh. In the absence of any fresh evidence, and without any sign of the vet or stable lad, it would be hopeless to attack him. The case was lost.

Just as Sir Crichton rose to begin questioning, Sir Desmond intervened and again addressed the judge. 'Might I, my lord, ask the court's indulgence? I realise that the normal procedure would be for my learned friend to cross-examine my client, which, having regard to the time, could best take plce after the midday adjournment. However, two of my witnesses, His Grace the Duke of Melton, and Sir Rowland Cull, have an important engagement tomorrow. I therefore wonder, if my learned friend has no objection, whether it would be possible to interrupt Mr Marsh's evidence at this stage, and call them as witnesses this afternoon. This would mean that my client would not be cross-examined until tomorrow, then Sir Crichton could have a fresh start ... ' he paused ... 'and have a whole day, if necessary, in front of him.'

The note of sarcasm in Sir Desmond's last observation was not lost on James, nor presumably on Sir Crichton or the judge.

'I have no objection Sir Desmond,' remarked the judge. 'But what does your opponent say?'

'I have none either, my lord,' Sir Crichton replied. 'On behalf of the defendants I'm quite happy to adopt the procedure suggested by my learned friend.'

'So be it. The cross-examination of Mr Marsh will be adjourned until tomorrow morning and the plaintiff can call his other witnesses. The court will now adjourn until 2.05 p.m.'

'All rise!' shouted the usher. But before the majority of those present could get to their feet Sir Reggie had disappeared, no doubt in the direction of the Inner Temple and his usual substantial lunch.

Outside court, James and Carlton, supported by Mr Twine, huddled in conference around Sir Crichton and his junior.

'Well,' said Sir Crichton, 'we have a slight stay of execution. Any news of that damned vet or that stable lad?'

'None, Sir Crichton,' answered Twine. 'Whilst in court this morning I received a note from my assistant Kennedy which says that our private investigators can't find hide nor hair of either of them. They're not at their homes. According to their neighbours they've both gone on holiday.'

Sir Crichton looked disappointed, but not particularly surprised. 'So then, young James, unless you turn up with something by 10.30 tomorrow it's down on our knees and grovel. It will stick in my throat because personally I don't like the cut of Mr Marsh's jib. Unfortunately he's gone down very well with the judge and I hate to think what the summing up will be like. But there it is. I'll see you back here at 2 p.m.'

James and Carlton crossed the Strand and went into the pub opposite the law courts. Two double whiskies failed to restore their confidence. Carlton was bending over backwards not to appear reproachful. But they both knew that the damages and costs which it now looked as if this case would entail could ruin the paper as well as James.

The lunch hour seemed to pass slowly. Carlton nibbled at a ham sandwich and flipped through a copy of the *Pacemaker*. He was silently reflecting how foolish he had been in persuading his proprietor to back this action. James tried to think of Gail but even that failed to cheer him up. He then thought of his mother and the financial difficulties which would lie ahead if he lost his job. Finally he remembered that losing his job meant the end of his participation in the nap competition and with it his £1000 bet, money which he didn't even have. He was beginning to feel very sorry for himself when Carlton pointed out that it was time to return to court.

On the resumption of the hearing, Sir Desmond first called on His Grace the Duke of Melton. His Grace, now well into his sixties and hard of hearing, had kept horses in training since his undergraduate days at Oxford and was a staunch supporter of National Hunt racing. He told the court that he had complete confidence and trust in his trainer's judgement and integrity. He had not seen the article himself on the morning of publication but someone, possibly his butler, had drawn it to his attention. Naturally he was concerned but had chosen to disbelieve it. He thought it was absolutely monstrous that a man such as Marsh should be pilloried in such a manner.

Sir Crichton then rose to cross-examine the distinguished witness. An unusual silence descended upon the court as he neatly arranged his papers and with a large red silk handkerchief cleaned his round gold-rimmed glasses. He had the benign air of a vicar at a parish tea party. His voice was clear and carrying, yet nonetheless gentle in tone.

'It would be right to say, your Grace, that racing can only survive if horses are run honestly and fairly according to the rules?'

'Of course.'

'That alas over the years there have been numerous occasions when those rules have been seriously breached?'

'I regret that that is true.'

'And sometimes those breaches have only been exposed as a result of investigations by newspapers?'

'Indeed.'

'And that in so doing, those newspapers have performed a great public service?'

'Yes, I fully accept that. But of course on this occasion ... '

'I'm sorry, your Grace, I'm not dealing with this occasion but with matters generally.'

'Yes, well ... '

'And that it is imperative for journalists, like the Jockey Club itself, to be alert to any possibility of dishonest conduct?'

'Of course.'

'Would you agree with me that if the contents of my client's article were susbstantially true then it would be quite proper to make those allegations contained in them public?'

'Yes, naturally I agree it would.' The Duke of Melton was becoming a little crusty.

'I'm obliged. Just one or two final questions, your Grace, on the issue of damages. You yourself disbelieved this article?'

'I did so on being reassured by my trainer.'

'So you've kept your horses with Mr Marsh?'

'That is correct. I've stood by him, as I hope any gentleman would.'

That was all right, thought James, as the duke ambled back to his seat among the spectators. The trouble is, it's all very well establishing the theory but it won't be of much use if we can't produce some facts in support of it.

In the event three other witnesses were called on behalf of the plaintiff. All spoke highly of Marsh's character and integrity as a trainer. Each in turn was cross-examined by Sir Crichton on the same lines, with responses similar to those elicited from the duke. By 3.45 the plaintiff had run out of witnesses, and much to James's relief it was decided to adjourn until the following day.

Outside court, on being told that there was no further news, Sir Crichton said shortly, 'I think we'd better all meet in my chambers tomorrow at 10.00 a.m. to decide the amount of money to offer by way of settlement. I've no doubt that Sir Desmond will strike a hard bargain and is bound to ask for all his not inconsiderable costs, £30,000 damages at least and a public apology. The problem is, the jury might easily give him more. Until tomorrow, then.' And with that he turned and walked down the long corridor towards the robing room, his silk gown and junior trailing after him.

James and Carlton walked gloomily back to Fleet Street, glad the *Sportsman* was one of the few newspapers which had not made the eastward trek to Wapping.

Eric Soper, who was helping out as the *Sportsman*'s court reporter was already typing up his account of the day's proceedings. James went and sat at the desk beside him. 'Well, what do you think? How's it going?'

'Quite frankly, bloody awfully. The judge and jury are eating out of old Desmond's hands. Your number's in the frame unless you can dig up some witnesses. Or do I gather they've already been declared non-runners?'

'Afraid it looks that way. We've got a couple of private detectives looking for them but we've virtually given up hope.'

'What's our own lawyer think? Funny looking bugger.'

'He's equally miserable. We've got to meet him tomorrow in his chambers to discuss the size of the offer.'

'Bad luck, matey. Still, you can't win 'em all.'

'That's what they said to Joan of Arc as they tied her to the stake.'

James returned to his desk and with a lot of effort got down to selecting tips for the next day's racing. He noticed on the wire that there was to be a memorial service at 11 a.m. for Sir Denby Croft, which was probably the important engagement due to occupy the time of the Duke of Melton and Sir Rowland Cull. At least Sir Denby, as a former owner of Morton Marsh's, couldn't come and speak up for him. James decided to return to his flat to make a few telephone calls to a couple of friendly jockeys in case they might have heard of the whereabouts of either Jackson or Milford. A ten thousand to one chance, he reckoned.

James walked slowly up the three flights of stairs to his flat, his mind on the next day's proceedings. As he opened the front door and reached for the light switch he almost failed to notice a scruffy brown envelope lying beside the empty milk bottles. He stopped, picked it up, and read his name printed in large capitals.

The flat was as cold as ever. Having turned on the boiler, he went in to the kitchen, switched on the kettle and made himself a cup of tea. Only then did he return to the package. It was a jiffy bag, re-used and sealed with Sellotape and a few staples. Sitting at the table he wrestled clumsily with the packaging. He had no idea what he would find inside. What finally fell out when the flap was torn open were two tapes of the kind used in a cassette recorder. There was no message of explanation or anything to identify the sender.

James moved to the sitting-room and slipped one of the tapes into his cassette machine. The first sound to emerge was of a phone being dialled; ringing tones followed, and the click of a receiver being lifted.

'Is that you, Jackson?' James recognised the voice at once. After all, he'd listened to it droning on smugly for part of the morning. It was Marsh's. 'I've got a runner on Saturday in the hurdle at Worcester. Spartacus.'

'Yeah?'

'Yes. And I want you to give him one of your special cocktails. By my reckoning if you do it on Friday afternoon all traces will have worn off by the time of the race.'

'That should be all right.' The voice had a sneering tone. 'But it'll cost you.'

'I know. I know. By the way, it worked a treat last time on Machiavelli. There'll be an extra £250 in it for

76

you if it all goes right this time.'

'Don't worry. This method's foolproof.'

The conversation ended. The rest of the tape was taken up with normal trivial conversations between Marsh and his owners and jockeys and domestic calls made by his wife. It was clear to James that somebody had been bugging Marsh's phone regularly.

James played the other tape. Once again it was full of ordinary everyday calls until, that is, the last one. This was Marsh's voice again and at its most matter-of-fact.

'Is that you, Cogan?'

'Yes.'

'Marsh here. Spartacus is off on Saturday and I want you to do the business for me. £3000 each way. And I don't want your boys making themselves obvious around the betting shops in the morning.'

'Right-ho, Mr Marsh, shall be done. Six monkeys each way.'

James thought for a moment. Who the hell was Cogan? And why was the name so familiar. He decided to call Victor Smiley, the chief racing tipster on the *London News* and the wisest old owl in the racing press room.

'Cogan? Sure I know Cogan. He's a bookmaker but he really makes his money out of commission betting. You know, putting on big bets for other punters and getting a slice of the winnings.'

James put down the phone. So it was true after all. But could he now persuade Sir Crichton?

Two hours later James was in the back of a taxi with Carlton and Mr Twine. They were on their way to Chester Square.

Mr Twine looked even more anxious than usual. 'I don't like it,' he said, shaking his head. 'I don't like it at all. Going like this to see Sir Crichton in his own home at 10 p.m.'

'I'm sure Sir Crichton will understand,' said Carlton cheerfully.

'Maybe. But it's most irregular and quite unusual. I've never done it before in forty years as a solicitor.'

'Well, Mr Twine, it's never too late to lose one's virginity.' Carlton for the first time seemed to be starting to enjoy himself.

'You did telephone Sir Crichton to tell him we were coming?' interrupted James in an attempt to save his lawyer's blushes.

'But of course. I explained that something urgent had come up and that it was quite essential to see him at once. I thought I'd leave the details to you.'

At that moment the taxi pulled up outside an impressive white-fronted house.

'Speaking for myself, I can't see any problem. After all we're paying him enough,' said Carlton, returning to the attack.

'Money has nothing to do with it. It's the principle of the thing. You only see counsel in their chambers.'

Carlton winked at James. Neither of them could resist a smile as Mr Twine reluctantly rang the bell.

Sir Crichton himself opened the door looking immaculate in a burgundy smoking jacket and dapper velvet slippers emblazoned with a pheasant. He couldn't have been more charming as he led the party into his study, the shelves of which were overflowing with books, none of which, James noticed with pleasure, seemed to have anything to do with the law — detective stories, P.G. Wodehouse, cricketing tales and biographies appeared to be Sir Crichton's literary poison. Having seated his visitors and dispensed bonhommie in the shape of large whiskies, he perched himself on the club fender, his back to the comforting fire, and invited James to tell him about the new development.

James recounted his discovery of the tapes. He then played the relevant passages on Sir Crichton's surprisingly sophisticated stereo, obviously designed more for Mozart than Marsh.

'Well, sir,' he said as the second one came to an end. 'Are we home and dry?'

Sir Crichton did not seem elated. Rather the reverse. 'Not quite, Mr Thackeray,' he replied. 'You see, we have two major problems. Firstly these tapes have been illegally obtained, by whoever left them at your flat. Phone bugging is a criminal offence unless authorised by the Home Secretary. Secondly, although the court is entitled to admit evidence that has been illegally obtained, it is at the discretion of the judge as to whether or not to allow it at this late stage to support a defence of truth. On present form I'm not optimistic. Old Reggie is eating out of Stanley's hands, and he positively purred as he took down Marsh's war record.'

'But surely public interest demands that this all come out?' objected Carlton.

'Public interest? Journalists always talk about public interest as if it is something they have on tap in the cellar. You must realise that there is a great difference between what is of genuine public interest and what is merely of interest to the public because it is scandalous.'

'Fair enough,' said James. 'But surely if he's crooked, Marsh ought to be exposed.'

'Well,' said Sir Crichton, 'we can only give it a try. But I must warn you now that if the judge allows it to be put in evidence and then Marsh denies that it is indeed his voice, then we are finished. And the damages will be enormous. You see, our problem is that we cannot call the makers of the tapes or any of the other parties to the telephone conversations. I don't somehow see Mr Cogan accepting a late-night commission from Mr Twine to give evidence tomorrow for us! Are the clients prepared to take this risk on damages?'

'That of course is a question for the proprietor and ... '

But before Mr Twine could finish and express any further view Carlton interrupted. 'I took the precaution of speaking to him on the phone in the South of France. He says that if you think it's worth it, Sir Crichton, we're to have a go and bugger the consequences. Do you?'

'Yes, I do think it's worth it, although personally I wouldn't describe the consequences quite so graphically. Another drink?'

Two whiskies later, the party left Sir Crichton's house. And James returned home to a lonely bed and a sleepless night.

Sir Reggie Bindworth was already mentally planning his summing up when at 10.35 the following morning Sir Crichton rose to cross-examine Morton Marsh. The reports of the case in the morning papers had ensured a packed house and the press box was overflowing. Some of the occupants had not even considered it necessary to bring their notebooks. The atmosphere was reminiscent of the big top and the arrival of the tightrope walker performing without a safety net.

Sir Crichton allowed his opening questions to be dealt with effortlessly.

'You pride yourself on your ability as a trainer?'

'Yes, it would be fair to say that.'

'You have over the last twenty years enjoyed enormous success?'

'A certain degree, I think I can say in all modesty.'

'Of course you've always regarded training as being as much a business as a sport?'

'I make my living from it.'

'Nonetheless you accept the need to play fair?'

'Yes.'

'You no doubt agree with everything his Grace the Duke of Melton said yesterday in evidence?'

'I endorse everything his Grace said.'

'And so you tell my lord and the jury that your horses have always run on their merits without any additional aids?'

'That is the case.'

'Presumably there are occasions when the services of a vet are required?'

'Obviously, Sir Crichton. For example, when a horse is injured or needs a vaccination.'

'I presume you have a regular vet?'

'Yes. Mr Lancaster of Lambourn.'

'And I presume that you use his services exclusively?'

'Correct, except when he's on holiday, when his partner Mr Osbert helps out.'

'There would therefore be no good reason for you to use any other vet?'

'Absolutely none that I can think of.'

'Do you know a vet called Jackson?'

'Jackson?'

'Yes, Jackson?'

'I think I've heard of some fellow of that name, but I don't know where he practises.'

'Have you ever had cause to use his services?'

'No, never.'

'Please reflect, Mr Marsh, before you answer. Can you think of any reason why you may have used his services in the past?'

'No, sir. I cannot and have not.'

'Did you in 1983 train a horse called Spartacus?'

'I did.'

'Did that horse have any injuries during the season?'

81

'No, he was a remarkably fit young hurdler.'

'So presumably there would have been no need to call in the services of a vet?'

'Quite right.'

'Did Spartacus win the Wackford Hurdle at Worcester on November 25th, 1983?'

'Yes.'

'Was he heavily backed?'

'I can't remember.'

'Well, let me remind you.' Sir Crichton held up a copy of the *Sportsman* and read from it. ' "Spartacus was heavily supported in the market and his odds fell from 11 to 1 to 9 to 2". '

'Really?'

'Yes, really, Mr Marsh, and it won by five lengths. Do you yourself ever bet?'

'Very rarely.'

'Did you have a bet on Spartacus?'

'Not that I can remember.'

'Or did you ask someone else to have a bet on your behalf, perhaps?'

'Certainly not.'

'So who do you think had the foresight to wager on the horse, owned, incidentally, by the Duke of Melton?'

'I have no idea. Unlike yourself, Sir Crichton, I cannot speak for other people.' By now Marsh's manner was becoming a trifle surly. Go on, thought James, get him.

'I suppose that you do a lot of business on the telephone?'

'Yes, naturally.'

'You'd have no difficulty in recognising your own voice?'

'What an absurd question. I have a very distinctive voice. I'd recognise it anywhere. I must say I fail to see the relevance of all these questions.'

'Patience, Mr Marsh, patience. Do you know a Mr Danny Cogan, who is, I believe a bookmaker and commission agent?'

'What is a commission agent?' interposed the judge. 'I can't follow this at all, Sir Crichton.'

'Someone, my lord, who places other people's bets on commission. Isn't that right, Mr Marsh?'

'So I've heard.'

At that stage Sir Crichton turned away from the witness box and faced the judge. 'My lord, I now wish to introduce some unusual evidence and since I anticipate an objection from my learned friend, I think it would be appropriate if your lordship were to consider the matter in the absence of both the jury and Mr Marsh.'

Sir Reggie, who had been doodling with his pen, was rather taken aback. 'This is all most unusual, but if your opponent has no objection, then ...'

Sir Desmond rose to his feet. 'Oh, none at all. I've been trying to follow my learned friend for the last half hour and can't wait for the great revelation now apparently in store.'

Once the jury and Marsh had left the courtroom Sir Crichton revealed the existence of the tapes, and without giving away their specific contents stated that they consisted of telephone conversations between Mr Marsh and third parties and asked leave of the judge to play them to Marsh when the cross-examination resumed. He admitted that the tapes must have been illegally obtained by parties unknown to the defendants. Notwithstanding, he submitted that justice demanded that the plaintiff be made to explain their contents. If he denied that it was his voice, or had a proper explanation for the conversations, which, on the face of it, revealed a flagrant breach of the rules of racing, then no doubt the jury would reflect those matters in their award of damages.

Sir Desmond protested. For over an hour he argued rationally, and at times passionately, for the rejection of the tapes. It was, he said, quite improper for the defendants to seek to introduce such evidence at such a late stage. At times the judge seemed disposed to agree with him, but Sir Crichton had the advantage of the last word and it tipped the scales.

'Public interest demands that the truth, however obtained, should come out at the hearing of an action,' the judge finally pronounced. 'Your clients, Sir Crichton, have no doubt been warned of the consequences if they are wrong.'

Marsh was recalled. Sir Crichton, looking more like a parson than ever, but now like a parson who has just discovered that a member of his congregation and two of the more mature choir-girls have been playing fast and loose with the seventh commandment, stared menacingly at the witness and began his attack.

'Mr Marsh, I am going to ask the usher to play a few seconds of a recording and I'd be grateful if you'd tell his lordship and the jury whether you recognise either of the voices.'

The usher then played the first few lines of the first tape.

'Did you recognise either voice, Mr Marsh?'

Marsh had gone rather pale. 'I'm not sure.'

'Then let the usher play it again for you.' Pause. 'Did that help this time?'

There was no answer from Marsh who looked pleadingly towards his counsel.

'That's your voice, isn't it? You are talking to a man called Jackson.'

'Yes, I think it is, but how ... '

'Let's now hear the rest of that conversation, Mr Marsh. I thought you said you didn't know Mr Jackson?'

'Well, yes, I must have been mistaken. It's easy to forget things but ... there's nothing there about betting.'

'Just hold on a minute, Mr Marsh. Listen to this second tape.'

Marsh's face went from pale to funereal grey as his conversation with Cogan was played to the court. There was a stunned silence among the gallery of spectators whilst the jurors looked at each other in astonishment and started whispering asides. Now it was Marsh who got the dirty look from Aunt Deidre.

Sir Desmond rose to his feet. 'Might I have a few moments alone with my client, my lord, outside court?'

'Yes, Sir Desmond, I think that would be appropriate. The court will now adjourn for ten minutes.'

Morton Marsh never returned to the witness box. On the resumption of the hearing, Sir Desmond told the court that in the light of the evidence his client had decided not to proceed any further with his claim.

Sir Crichton rose slowly to his feet and politely asked the judge for a verdict to be entered for the defendants, with costs.

'So be it,' sighed Sir Reggie Bindworth, and looking at his watch left the court. He calculated that he would have time for lunch at the Garrick and a couple of frames of snooker before facing his wife and sister-in-law.

Sir Crichton Blade shook James and Carlton warmly by the hand. James in turn congratulated his counsel.

Suddenly Gail was by their side. 'You were wonderful!' she said to Sir Crichton, and to James's amusement and Mr Twine's astonishment, kissed him on the cheek.

85

Sir Crichton made no attempt to rub away the lipstick smudge. He was delighted. 'I take it you're connected with this young man? Please make sure in future that he doesn't come with such a late run. It's far too hard on the nerves!'

The congratulations over, James and Carlton walked the few hundred yards to El Vino's, where several of the *Sportsman*'s hacks were certain to be refreshing themselves. Gail had to return to her office and left reluctantly, but promised to cook James a victory supper that night.

Three hours and four bottles of champagne later, James could be seen being carried into a taxi to be taken home. It was with great difficulty that he crawled upstairs to his flat and found the lock with his key. As he lurched inside the phone was ringing. He answered it. 'Thackeray? Chief Superintendent Pale here, Scotland Yard. We met briefly at Newbury in Inspector Hardcastle's office. I hear you've been taping people's phone conversations. It strikes me that your constant presence at the scene of the crime needs some explaining. Tomorrow, here, at the Yard. 9.30 a.m.'

James put the phone down and passed out.

Chapter 9

The walk, or more accurately the trek, to Chief Superintendent Pale's room involved climbing numerous flights of stairs and tramping along what seemed interminable corridors. It was more, James imagined, like the headquarters of the BBC than of the greatest police force in the world. He could not resist asking his guide, a young police constable, what he thought of the chief superintendent.

'I don't think it's my position to comment on my superiors, sir.'

'Yes, of course, quite right, officer. Just that I'm not used to this sort of thing and was hoping you could reassure me.'

'All I can tell you is that the Chief Superintendent is regarded as one of the toughest men on the Force.'

It was in consequence a very nervous James who was left outside a door marked simply '827'. He knocked, and a deep voice rasped 'Enter'.

Pale rose from behind his desk and shook him firmly by the hand. James looked at the Chief Superintendent. He had hardly been given an opportunity to take in his features at their brief and somewhat embarrassing meeting at Newbury police station.

He put Pale in his early fifties. He was distinctly overweight with a very chubby face reminiscent of a pug. God seemed to have overlooked the need for a neck, and Pale's head sat squarely on the white collar of his shirt. James declined the offer of a cigarette and while Pale lit his own he glanced at the two framed black-and-white photographs on his desk. Each contained a half-length picture of an ugly and aggressive male, with a number stamped on his chest.

Pale caught James's glance and smiled. 'Not my family, Mr Thackeray. Those two were the leaders of the Mitcham Machete Gang and they are now holidaying at Her Majesty's Government's expense in Parkhurst. A very nasty pair of individuals who took particular pleasure in collecting their victims' ears. Till I captured this mob I never realised that ears came in so many different shapes and sizes. I keep those photographs there to remind me what the job's really about.'

'Good God!' said James, starting to play with his right earlobe.

The chief superintendent walked over to one of the large filing cabinets lining the room. He's going to get out the machete now, thought James. What he removed, however, was a large manila file. Returning to his desk, he asked James, 'Do you think George Weatherby killed Denby Croft?'

'No, I don't.'

'Nor do I, although he had the obvious motive. There's something about it I don't like. It sticks in my throat.' James couldn't see any place on Pale's body for such a luxury, but he nodded in agreement nonetheless. 'Now tell me, Mr Thackeray, about the discovery of those tapes.'

James described how he had discovered the tapes outside his flat on returning home from court and admitted he had no idea who had made them or left them there.

Pale didn't seem surprised. 'In that case we know a little, although not much, more than you. We had Mr Marsh in here last night for a chat. We suspected that he might have been blackmailed and that the blackmailers had released the tapes when he refused to cough up any more. He's a tough bastard, though, and couldn't or wouldn't help us.'

'Have you checked his house?'

'We're not that slow, Mr Thackeray. While he was here we examined all the phones down at his training establishment at Lambourn and found an eavesdropping device in the receiver of the one in his office. With the right equipment his conversations could be picked up within a four-mile radius. Of course, we've no idea just how long it's been there.' Pale stood up and started to pace the room. 'It struck me that if someone bugged Marsh's phone they could just as easily have bugged Sir Denby's. That would explain the curious note we found on him on the day of his murder.'

Pale walked up to James and looked him straight in the eye. His breath smelt of stale tobacco. 'I think we're dealing with a gang of sophisticated blackmailers and how I look at it is that they can win both ways. If they overhear decent racing information they can use it. If they hear the caller is up to no good they can blackmail him. Our problem is going to be finding a victim who will talk – unlike Mr Marsh, who is alive and won't or Sir Denby Croft, who is dead and can't.'

'Do you think, Chief Superintendent,' James asked with a show of diffidence, 'that I could perhaps see the note which was found on Sir Denby?'

'I don't see why not. It's with the exhibit bundle downstairs.'

Pale pressed the buzzer on his intercom and called for the Croft exhibits. Three minutes later a pretty uniformed policewoman appeared with a large plastic bag. James watched her leave the room and wondered whether she was wearing stockings or merely black tights.

Pale had other things on his mind. He handed James the blackmail note. 'Say anything to you?'

James studied the piece of cardboard with the words cut from newspaper glued upon it. 'No, except that whoever compiled this reads the *Sportsman*. I recognise the type face. I suspect the reference to cheating could be to the bad running of Paradise Lost the time before it won at Newbury. It was at Huntingdon, and other people besides myself felt something funny was going on.'

Pale took another piece of paper out of the plastic bag and pushed it over towards James. 'O.K. Now can you enlighten us about this? It's the betting slip that the police constable found on the floor of the horsebox near the body. We think it must have been dropped by Croft, or perhaps more likely by his killer. Weatherby, of course, denies knowing anything about it. But as everyone in racing apparently knows, he's a huge gambler.'

'And a very shrewd one,' observed James. 'Can I make a note of these selections? I wonder whether you could lend me a sheet of paper and possibly a pencil?'

Pale gave him a mocking look. 'I heard times were

90

hard in Fleet Street. No note-book?'

James ignored him and wrote down the selections which had been typed out on the betting slip:

Newbury
    1.30 Menelek For Ever
    2.00 I'm All Right Jack
    2.30 Paradise Lost
    3.30 Archimedes

'Paradise was a winner, but I can't remember what happened to the other three. My mind, as you'll appreciate, wasn't really on racing that day.'

'Perhaps you could find out for me? The Newbury boys have rather overlooked this line of enquiry since arresting Weatherby, and my own interest at the moment is still unofficial. You mix with the racing crowd, so if you hear about anyone in sudden financial difficulties or behaving strangely, give us a call.' James reflected that Pale's description would fit most of his friends. 'Here's my home phone number, Thackeray. You can ring me any time day or night. My wife's used to it.'

It seemed strange to hear that Pale was married. James had pictured him as being wedded to the Force, but if that WPC was anything to go by, the prospect was not so unattractive. He thought it only right to tell Pale about Paddy and what he might have seen that day.

'It probably isn't anything,' said Pale, 'but I'll have my boys look into his present whereabouts.'

James chose not to mention the call from Willie Angell. He thought that information was better coming from Mrs Rivers and he couldn't wholly forget his mother's anxieties about the dangers of helping the police with their enquiries.

Chapter 10

That night James and Gail sat down in his flat and went through the racing results for 25th November. It soon emerged that the owner of the mysterious betting slip was either extremely shrewd or an extremely lucky punter. His first selection, trained by Morton Marsh, had won at odds of 5 to 2. His second, also trained by Marsh, had started as even money favourite and been beaten by a short head in a photo finish. Paradise Lost, of course, had flown in at 7 to 1 and Archimedes, also trained by Archie Duncan, had pulled off a surprise victory at 33 to 1. It had been ridden by Willie Angell and not the stable jockey Phil Hope.

'Is that unusual, James?' asked Gail.

'Pretty, unless of course Duncan had another runner in the same race. Hold on while I have a look. Yes, here it is, Ever Watchful. Let's see what the RACEFORM notes say. "Fourth behind Archimedes. Always in with a chance. Couldn't quicken on run in". It started at 7 to 2, and that explains Archimedes's long odds. It happens now and again and it's very embarrassing for a trainer when his less fancied runner comes home. You'll probably find Angell had ridden it in its other races when Phil Hope was riding elsewhere, and without Duncan knowing it, had given it a pull.'

'Isn't that against the rules?'

James laughed and gave Gail's hair a playful tug. 'He's not called The Ancient Mariner because he likes the sea!'

Then another thought struck him. 'Look,' he went on, 'there's racing at Plumpton on Thursday and according to the four-day declarations, our Willie's got a ride booked in the fifth. I think I might go and ask him one or two pertinent questions. I can drive down there after I've ridden out on The Sportsman at Duncan's.'

'For God's sake, be careful. We've got no evidence against Angell, and you'll find yourself being stopped if you start poking your nose into other people's business.'

'All right. I promise to be careful, scout's honour!' James crossed his fingers and thought how he'd hated scouts anyway.

'Right,' said Gail. 'We've sorted out your problem. Now can we have a go at solving mine?'

The idea of Gail having any problems had never occurred to James. She had always been reluctant to talk about her past and he had chosen not to ask inquisitive questions. Experience had long taught him that you often get unpalatable answers. 'Fire away!' he said.

'It's about my job.' James felt pleased. For a ghastly

moment, he thought that a former Mr Right had reappeared on the scene. 'Working for the literary agent is great fun and the people are very nice, but frankly the pay's lousy, and I don't have much money over after paying the rent and getting essentials. The thing is, I'd really like to be able to buy you the odd present and pay my way when we go out to dinner or the cinema. You're broke, and can't afford to pay for both of us all the time.'

James was touched by her generous thoughts. 'But do you really enjoy what you're doing? That's the only thing that counts.'

'You know I do, but look at you. You had to give up your dream of being a trainer when your father died.'

'But that was different. I had a mother and sister to support, and anyway, I still managed to stay in racing. Who knows, I might still become a trainer some day. As for you paying your way, look at all the things you do for me. If you're happy at work, I'm happy. If I were you, I'd stick at it. Just wait till you discover some famous author!'

'I suppose you're right. Pass me the manuscript over there in my briefcase, and I'll get cracking. The only problem is that this one's about the homosexual practices of some South American tribe. I think they're now extinct.'

'That sounds logical.'

'Hardly the stuff bestsellers are made of!'

'You never know!' replied James.

94

Chapter 11

Archie Duncan could not have been more friendly. This was the young journalist's third visit to his yard but on both previous occasions Duncan had been over in Ireland looking for potential 'chasers. As they walked together over to The Sportsman's box, Archie, who was elegantly clad in fawn jodhpurs and brightly polished leather riding boots, shouted instructions to his well-disciplined staff. The atmosphere pulsed with efficiency and success.

'I'll be honest with you, James. When I was told that Sir Randolph was giving The Sportsman away in a competition I thought he was barmy. When I heard you were going to ride him I was convinced he'd lost his marbles. Still, he pays the training fees and after seeing you ride the other week at Kempton, I think you've got the makings of a jockey. You ride a bit long and are rather untidy in a finish, but otherwise not too bad.'

By now they had reached The Sportsman's box and Duncan and James were stroking the animal's head. Duncan told the lad to saddle him up and bring him out. As he led him out of the box the stirrup iron caught on the door-post.

'Be careful, you idiot,' shouted Duncan, momentarily losing his composure. He helped James into the saddle. 'None of this overweight business on my fellow in the National, please!'

'Don't worry,' replied James. 'My girlfriend has put me on one of these new scientific diets. I think it's called starvation.'

The Sportsman worked well over five furlongs and James popped him over three schooling fences. The horse jumped effortlessly and James was impressed by the accurate way he measured his fences.

Over breakfast he met Mrs Duncan and her two teenage daughters, Clare and Lucy. They were her children by her first marriage, her husband having died four years before in a hunting accident. The atmosphere was not easy, as Duncan's earlier good humour rapidly disappeared and he set about criticising his wife for everything under the sun.

'Have you sent off those entries yet for Cheltenham and Haydock?' he barked.

'No, darling, I'll make sure they go off this morning.'

'Why must you always leave it so late? You know how short staffed we are at the moment. I can't do everything myself, you know.'

'I'm sorry, dear, but ... '

'Don't bore me with your excuses. I don't want young James here to think we're running an inefficient show. He might go off and tell his employer, and bang goes a good owner.'

James said nothing, and Mrs Duncan tried valiantly to change the conversation.

'Where are you off to today, James?'

'I'm going to Plumpton. Not a very exciting card, I'm afraid. And what about you, sir?' James directed his question respectfully to his trainer.

'I've got to stay here to take delivery of five horses from Morton Marsh's yard. Your libel victory brought me a couple of new owners, I'm afraid I have to admit. You won't go writing anything nasty about me, I hope?'

'I think ruining one trainer is enough for a lifetime. What do you think of Willie Angell?'

'As a jockey? He's all right. He's a good horseman. I occasionally put him up on one of my horses if Phil is riding elsewhere and it's too difficult a ride for one of the apprentices. Why do you ask?'

'Nothing, really. He knows a mutual friend, that's all, and I was hoping to have a chat with him at Plumpton today.'

Mrs Duncan looked at the clock. 'You'd better get going. It'll take you a couple of hours to get there and I heard on the radio there are road works on the M 25.'

'Even longer,' said Clare, 'if that old banger outside is your motor!'

Happily the old Morris was not a sensitive creature and took James steadily through Berkshire and Surrey into Sussex, where they soon reached Plumpton. It was a filthy day and as James waited at the level crossing by the side of the entrance, he could see the rain sweeping over the Downs less than two miles away, and falling in sheets over the racecourse itself.

Set on the inside of a moderately steep hill, and just over a mile in circumference, the tight left-handed track is a jockey's nightmare when the ground is firm and little better than just a bad dream in conditions like today's. Too many horses with too little room to get a clear view of the fences is one of the two reasons why Plumpton seldom appears on any jockey's list of favourite courses. The other is the downhill run on the back straight with its three tricky fences. On dry ground even normally slow horses managed to reach speeds beyond their trainers' wildest dreams, but they were speeds at which few could jump safely.

James felt renewed gratitude that today his role was purely that of a spectator. That, at least, was what he told himself, but in his heart he knew that he would leap at the offer of a spare ride. It might even improve his own unimpressive record here: two rides, two falls.

Only the hardened punters and those with a vested interest came to Plumpton on days like this, pretty course though it was, and James counted barely more than a score of passengers alighting from the race train, heads lowered into the southerly winds as they fought their way towards the course.

Soon the large wooden railway gates moved slowly back, allowing the old Morris to bump forward over the line before turning right onto the grit track that crossed the course itself and led to the car park in the centre in front of the stands.

He locked the car and crossed to the other side of the course to the bar for a glass of beer and a sandwich. The rain was still pelting down and since Willie Angell didn't have a ride until the fifth race, where he was on the favourite, Shadow Boxer, James decided to watch the other races from the stands, without going to see the runners parading in the paddock first. He hoped that Willie was successful. A victory, he calculated, might just sweeten him up sufficiently to part with a bit of information about Paddy.

James watched the runners in the first four races slog their way through the bottomless ground and finish absolutely legless. Two of the races were won by horses trained under permit and James imagined that they probably did their training gallops in fields around a farm somewhere, instead of on carefully maintained gallops like most of the others. They would be well suited to the heavy going.

He decided to brave the rain to watch as the runners for Willie's race walked round the paddock. On paper there were only two who had a chance, but in conditions like these the form book could not be counted on. Shadow Boxer looked as well as could be expected for a horse that was soaking wet, which was more than could be said for the girl who was leading him round.

He watched until the jockeys had mounted and then returned to his position at the top of the grandstand to watch the runners canter past to the two and a half mile start situated at the bottom of the home straight next to the railway line. As the horses came by, it wasn't difficult to pick out those with the high knee action which would be suited by the soft ground. James put eight out of the seventeen runners in this category, including Shadow Boxer, but the remainder were having difficulty even at a canter.

Five minutes later, the race was under way. For a novice chase at Plumpton the first circuit was something of a miracle, with not a single horse falling. Shadow Boxer had not put so much as a foot wrong at any of the seven fences and Willie had him perfectly positioned on the inside, just behind the leaders. Then just as they jumped the fence past the stands with less than a circuit to go James noticed something odd. Instead of pulling off the rail as his horse rounded the top bend, and thus avoiding a horse in front of him that was obviously tiring, Willie stayed where he was and went from fifth to tenth place as a succession of horses went past him. It looked as if this was going to be the one in three which had earned the jockey his nickname.

That suspicion was confirmed by what happened at the first of the three downhill fences on the far side, the point where jockeys with any chance set sail for home. Here Willie deliberately forced Shadow Boxer to make a mistake by getting him too close to the fence at take-off while at the same time pulling the horse's head to one side so that he was unable to arch his back and jump properly. By the time Shadow Boxer had recovered his balance on the landing side, unaided by Willie, he had lost at least another five lengths and his chance of winning looked remote. James could not resist shaking his head in admiration at Willie's skill. What he had just witnessed was beyond the capabilities of most jockeys, and there was no doubt that if Willie had not been crooked he could have been one of the top riders.

Now, as the horses galloped towards the middle of the downhill fences, Shadow Boxer began to gain ground on the leaders and this time was too quick even for Willie. He took off to jump a whole stride too soon and put in an enormous leap which landed him as far the other side of the fence and back within six lengths of the leader. James smiled to himself, and wondered what Willie was thinking of his mount's reluctance to be an accomplice in villainy.

At the last fence on the far side, the open ditch, Shadow Boxer did the same thing again, and from the stands he appeared to be going the best of all the runners. Now there were only four furlongs to go and James felt relieved that from now on it would be impossible for Willie to prevent the horse from winning, short of jumping off him. But Willie was to prove him wrong. As the horses in front of him rounded the bottom bend, and headed towards the fence adjacent to the railway line, Willie, with acres of room on his outside, tried to force Shadow Boxer through a non-existent gap between the running rail and the horse immediately in front. It was a miracle he stayed on board as his horse cannoned into the white plastic and all but fell over as he lost his balance. Willie deserved an Oscar for the way he snatched Shadow Boxer up and switched to the outside, his whip flailing, riding as though the'devil himself were after him. But those lost lengths could not be made up, and Shadow Boxer had to be content with a fast finishing second place.

As they made their way back to the unsaddling enclosure a couple of punters started hurling abuse at Willie, but it was obvious from his abstracted expression that their insults were like water off a duck's back. The jockey's thoughts were almost certainly on the hard-luck story he was going to give the waiting owner and trainer and the large packet or readies he could expect from the real source of his riding instructions.

James waited until the jockeys had gone out for the last race before slipping into the changing room. Fortunately the valets were in the drying room collecting the breeches from the earlier races, and were no doubt looking forward to a quick getaway from the course at the end of a long day. The other riders in the fifth race had quickly changed to go home. Willie, who had lingered to report to his mount's connections, was now sitting alone in the corner and in the process of taking off his racing sweater. There was still some mud on his forehead and his breeches were filthy. He was tall for a jockey, even a National Hunt one. He had a long scar down the side of his right cheek and his eyes were a good deal too close together for James's liking.

'What d'you want in here? I know you!' he shouted. 'You're the little shit who writes all the rude things about me! Get out!'

'It won't take long. Yes, I'm James Thackeray from

the *Sportsman*. I understand that you might have seen a friend of mine some time before Christmas. Paddy Develera. He's a lad in Monty Spry's yard. He's gone missing and naturally his friends are worried.'

'Are they now? Well, I can't help you. I've never heard of the man. Who did you say he worked for?'

'Monty Spry at Compton.'

The tone of Willie Angell's voice became extremely caustic. 'Oh, not one of the trainers who retains my services. I suspect your friend, he's Irish by the sound of it, has gone back to the bog from which he sprang. So why don't you go back to your office and be a pain in someone else's backside?'

'Charmingly put, Willie,' retorted James. 'But before I do, just tell me one thing. When you won on Archimedes at Newbury, were you surprised?' With which parting question he slipped out of the door just as Willie Angell's riding boot slammed against the wall.

Chapter 12

The following Sunday Gail and James drove down to East Hendred to see Mrs Rivers. There was still no news of Paddy. She told them the police had already been down to interview her and had made a thorough search of his room. It had not taken them long. As she confided, the Irishman was not a great man for possessions. Most of his money went on board and lodging and backing what he called his certainties.

As they sat in the cosy living room it seemed a strange thought that Paddy might never be coming back. Of course, it was possible that the secretive Irishman would suddenly turn up out of the blue, working for some new trainer, but James was beginning to doubt it. As for poor Mrs Rivers, her dilemma was painful. She could not bring herself to let out Paddy's room, yet her lodgers were her only source of income. James found himself writing out a cheque for fifty pounds to help tide her over. At first she proudly refused to accept his money, but she relented when he told her, falsely, that he would reclaim it from his newspaper.

On Monday, racing was cancelled because of the bad weather. It was thus a good day for James to contact Chief Superintendent Pale, which he had decided to do.

Arriving at the Yard, he found the Chief in sombre mood. 'Why didn't you tell us about Paddy's meeting with this jockey fellow Angell? You must have realised that his landlady would have let it out when we saw her?'

'I'm sorry. I know I should have done but I wanted to have a word with Willie first.'

'I expect you found him unco-operative.'

'That's putting it mildly. He threw a boot at me as I left the jockeys' changing room.'

'That sounds in character. He was bloody rude to our boys when they visited him last Friday to discuss his movements on the night your Irishman disppeared. He says he was at home all evening with his wife, recovering from a nasty fall at the races earlier that afternoon. She's a pretty disagreeable woman and confirms his story. And before you say anything we've checked the racecourse and he *did* have a nasty fall that day.'

'Perhaps Paddy has gone home to Ireland after all?'

'It's possible, but I don't believe it. We've been on to the Irish police and apparently they want him for questioning about some money that disappeared from his old employers in Dublin, about £2000. Of course, as they say, he could be anywhere down by the south coast by now, and with very little chance of being discovered. Anything else?'

'Yes. I looked up the selections on that betting slip for you.'

'Well?'

'Two of the runners were trained by Morton Marsh and the other two by Archie Duncan. Three winners and one beaten favourite doesn't sound like an amateur punter to me. What if the villains were tapping Duncan's phone as well as Marsh's?'

'Could be. And that, of course, if it's true, would explain how they got their information about Sir Denby. Yes, the more I think about it the more I think you may be right. So I reckon we'll get on and check out Duncan's phone for a bug. There's a chance of course that it could have been removed by now. But with a bit of luck we'll still be one step ahead of the game.'

'Is there anything else I can do, Chief Superintendent?'

'Not for the moment. But we'll let you know if you can.'

James rose from his chair. He walked towards the door and was just about to open it when Pale called him back.

He turned, expecting a friendly word of caution. 'Next time you come, remind me to show you that machete!' Pale said, and grinned at his discomfort.

Chapter 13

February James devoted to the grim task of losing weight. Archie had made it clear that he expected The Sportsman's jockey to be able to go to scales under eleven stone if necessary, and there was certainly no point arguing with the man who was currently leading the trainer's table and had every chance and intention of still being there at the end of the season.

With an almost demonic relish Gail had devised a bran-based diet which made James doubt whether there was a life before death, and every morning he could be seen ashen-faced and weighed down by pullovers, chasing the determined throng of joggers who trundled round Hyde Park. The evening cocktail in his flat had given way to the less homely atmosphere of a sauna near Piccadilly where he watched the beads of sweat jump like lemmings from his paunch and marvelled at the candour and boldness of his fellow occupants in discarding their towels.

On a happier note The Sportsman gained his second successive win, this time at Wincanton. Everybody was delighted with the way the horse had attacked his fences and even though he only won by a fast-diminishing head, the omens were good for Aintree. Archie seemed pleased, although James thought he overheard him saying to a fellow trainer that he would be more confident if he had a proper jockey on his back on the big day.

Unfortunately the handicapper had also noticed the improvement in form and when the National weights were announced at the end of the month he had allotted the horse eleven stone two. Archie was none too happy, but at least it meant that James had four pounds less to lose – or, as he put it, one hundred fewer mouthfuls of cereal and two hundred fewer circuits of Hyde Park.

There was still no news of Paddy and James had even gone to the expense of putting an advertisement in an Irish newspaper asking for information about his whereabouts. His lad's racing passport was still at Monty Spry's yard and without it he could not get another job in racing. Gordon, the head lad, had made it clear in no uncertain terms what he would do with it if Paddy turned up to reclaim it. As far as Chief Superintendent Pale was concerned the Irishman's name would just have to be added to the thousands of people who inexplicably go missing every year.

James consoled himself with the hope that he might turn up at the annual Festival at Cheltenham in March, the mecca of all National Hunt enthusiasts, which includes half the Irish population, and where he himself had been booked to ride an outsider in the big amateurs' race on the Thursday, the last day of the meeting.

To add icing to the cake James had also received a surprise invitation from the proprietor of his paper to dine and stay the night before the race. Each year Sir Randolph threw a large house party for the races at his beautiful Elizabethan manor house, Raleighs, set in its own parkland some twenty miles from the course. His hospitality on these occasions was legendary but, as far as the *Sportsman*'s staff were concerned, based solely on hearsay. Only Carlton had ever received an invitation, and it appeared that this year it had either gone astray or he had been jocked off in his junior's favour. In either event the editor was not best pleased.

It was well past 7.30 p.m. when James's Morris Traveller turned through the wrought-iron gates and began its sedate journey along the drive which led to the house. He was late because he had stayed behind after the races to telephone through his copy and selections for the following day. The news of his invitation had provoked plenty of jokes at the office, including the offer of two codpieces, and Eric Soper had made a point of talking to him after his copy had been dictated and asking him to bring back some loo paper, which was alleged to come from Harrods and to bear the proprietor's family crest.

As the Morris chuntered along the drive flanked by oak trees James felt increasingly excited. He was not averse to the occasional bit of luxury and was also curious to see what the gossip columnists in the popular press had dubbed Sir Randy's love nest. The latter had already shaken off two wives in highly publicised, and in the first case lurid, circumstances and would now in golfing terms be five off the tee. No doubt there would be some glamorous blonde with a magnificent chest playing hostess tonight, preferably in a low-cut evening dress. James's foot slipped on the clutch as his fantasies took wing. She would, of course, insist on seducing him, and since his employer would be urging him on, he would have no option but to obey. At least, that was what he would tell Gail!

After nearly two miles, during which James had been expecting to see it round every corner, the house suddenly appeared out of the darkness. It certainly lived up to expectations. Arc lamps on the lawn illuminated the timbered brown and white façade, and a blaze of light from innumerable windows created the impression of a majestic ocean-going liner with a party in progress in every cabin. He parked the Morris beside a gleaming green Bentley.

Relish, the butler, opened the front door, and carrying James's scruffy canvas bag – Gail had been right, he should have taken his father's old leather case – showed him up the ornately carved double staircase to his room on the first floor. With that perfect blend of deference and weariness which is the hallmark of his calling, Relish informed him that he was the last to arrive and that the other guests were already changing for dinner, which would be served in three-quarters of an hour. James took this as a mild rebuke, and forgetting to ask where the bathroom was, decided to dress as quickly as possible. He thought for a moment of ingratiating himself by passing on a certainty which he had been given for the last race on tomorrow's card, but on reflection dropped this idea. His canvas bag might easily be taken as evidence that his tipping skills were less than lucrative.

Having washed and shaved in the basin in the corner he paused briefly to enjoy the surroundings. The huge four-poster bed was draped in chintz to match the curtains and boded well for a peaceful night's sleep. If only, James thought, Gail was there to share it with him. But she probably would not have agreed. Why, he wondered, did she find him so resistible?

James tied his black bow tie after two or three shots, eased himself into his father's ancient dinner jacket, and nonchalantly sprinkled a hint of after-shave, a Christmas present from his sister, on his cheeks. Looking into the full-length mirror he was not displeased with what he saw. According to Gail, the double-breasted look was now right back in fashion, although he was a trifle uneasy about the trousers, which were baggy enough to accommodate a set of golf clubs.

Flexing his upper lip and putting on his best American drawl he snarled out loud, 'Here's looking at you kid!' and turned around, ready to throw himself into the evening ahead.

The sight of Relish staring poker-faced at him from the threshold took him aback.

'I'm sorry to disturb you, sir, but I did knock and the door was open.'

James swallowed his embarrassment. 'Just doing my Humphrey Bogart bit!'

'Of course you were, sir. I was just wondering what time you would like your morning tea?'

'I've got to leave early to have a sauna in Cheltenham, so would seven o'clock be all right?'

'Certainly. Mr Duncan has also asked for it at that time.'

James perked up. 'Mr Duncan the trainer? Is he here as well? That's good news. And Mrs Duncan?'

'Just Mr Duncan. I understand that his wife has stayed behind to supervise their training establishment. Unless there is something else, sir, I must return to the other guests downstairs.'

'No. No, thank you very much ... er ... ' James hesitated. 'Relish.'

He almost found himself saying 'sir'.

Sir Randolph greeted him warmly as he came down

the stairs. For a man in his late fifties the newspaper magnate was remarkably well preserved and James wondered whether the full head of dark hair was a miracle of science or of nature. He made a mental note to ask Eric Soper, the office sage on such matters, when he next saw him.

Sir Randolph speedily introduced him to some of the other members of the party. Looking round, James counted thirteen guests besides himself, all dressed to the nines and drinking different sorts of cocktails. For one who had no difficulty in remembering the name and pedigree of any four-legged animal as well as its starting price, if not Tote odds, James was strangely helpless when confronted by the two-legged variety. His attempts to join in the conversation of one or two groups went virtually unnoticed, although one guest, evidently mistaking him for one of the staff, asked for 'a martini, shaken not stirred'. It was with some relief that he spotted Archie Duncan over in a corner of the hall, beside a statue of a cupid firing off a love dart, and deep in conversation with an extremely attractive woman whose complexion suggested that she might be Latin American. He was moving towards them when he was suddenly grabbed by an overweight and well-rounded woman with greying hair, bedecked in what was no doubt priceless jewellery.

After a few sentences it was clear to James that Lady Bellweather – 'You can call me Leonora, dear' – had found a new victim upon whom to inflict her life story, and had no intention of letting him go. She had reached the property crash of 1973 when he somehow managed to turn the subject to horse racing, but even then she was an authority on breeding, training and probably, James suspected, all-weather gallops. At present, she and her husband had five horses in training with Monty Spry – but at this stage her voice dropped to a confidential tone – she was seriously thinking of moving them to that wonderful man, Archie Duncan. He really had been so witty and charming over dinner the night before, and she quite refused to believe the racecourse gossip that he treated his wife very badly. He looked too nice a man for that.

Murmuring agreement, James glanced round the room in an attempt to work out who was Sir Randy's latest lover. The good-looking girl talking to Duncan was an obvious candidate, with her mouth-watering figure and what looked like Betty Grable legs.

Lady Bellweather saw his inquisitive look and took it as an invitation to provide a curriculum vitae on each of their fellow guests. It transpired that these included five married couples, all the men being either wealthy industrialists or city financiers. At least two had household names. The girl still talking to Archie was a former Peruvian beauty queen, whose elderly husband had recently died, leaving her a fortune. Now she was throwing herself into London society – and that's not all, added Leonora in a whisper. The only other unattached woman was older, yet still very attractive, a former debutante who had recently divorced her husband. Lady Bellweather tapped her glass knowingly and mouthed the word 'Drink'. James was uncertain whether it was the wife's or the husband's problem, but in any event, the under-butler, Cave, merely took it as an invitation to refill their glasses with champagne.

James was by now beginning to feel extremely peckish. Discreet whisperings between Relish and Sir Randolph suggested that dinner was ready to be served, but that Cook was throwing a wobbler in the kitchen. Making a feeble excuse about talking riding tactics, James broke away from his lecturer's vocal grasp and joined Archie in the corner. Coincidentally, or so James hoped, the Peruvian chose this moment to go and chat to her host, and the affectionate and playful way in which she slipped her arm through his, confirmed James's guess that she was the flavour of the month.

Archie Duncan was in exceptionally high spirits after two days of the Festival meeting. He already had two winners and a second, and with his stable in such form, he was beginning to nurse hopes for his runner in the next day's Gold Cup. He was busy going through the respective merits of the opposition when James looked up and caught his first glimpse of the fifteenth guest coming slowly and confidently down the stairs. In a red silk gown, she looked immensely attractive, her long dark hair caressing her half-naked shoulders. The gleaming sapphire set amidst the pearl choker which adorned her neck made Lady Bellweather's ornaments look like cheap prizes from a fair ground. This, James thought to himself, is real class.

'She's quite something, isn't she?' commented Archie.

'She certainly is,' replied James. 'I didn't know that Sir Randolph knew Lady Croft.'

'Oh yes, he's known Clarissa for years, well before she met and married old Denby. In fact, it was Clarissa who introduced Randolph to me as a trainer.'

'That's all news to me, although I suppose there's no reason why I should know. She seems to have recovered from her husband's death, then?'

'Don't be taken in by her appearance. This house party is her first public outing since the tragedy and she's still very upset. She's putting on a brave face, but in her case it's done with a lot of style.'

'I hear they were a very close couple.'

'Absolutely devoted to each other. After the death of his first wife, and with no children, Sir Denby was very low, but then old Clarissa came along like a breath of fresh air and instilled new life into him. I just hope they hurry up and put that bastard Weatherby inside for as long as possible.'

James grunted in what sounded like agreement. This was certainly not the time or place to air his own theories.

Dinner lived up to all James's expectations. He devoured five courses in blissful contempt of his diet, comforting himself with the knowledge that he only had to ride at twelve stone in the next day's race and there was also the pleasure of the sauna ahead in the morning. Seated in the very middle of the long dining table, he had unfortunately drawn the short straw and found Lady Bellweather on his right. She proceeded to pick up on her life story from where James had hoped it had been left for good in 1973. She regaled him with her husband's rise from the ashes of bankruptcy to wealth and power and eventually a peerage. Although he had made his fortune in retailing, he now devoted himself, as did she, to charitable works, in the process abandoning the Labour Party because of 'all those loony lefties'.

James could not resist looking down the table at the rotund figure of Lord Bellweather as he knocked back the claret as if it were tapwater. He had obviously become a Social Democrat.

As the evening progressed Clarissa Croft became more and more animated.

She soon forgot the role of grief-stricken widow and told a string of hilarious anecdotes about her trip the previous year to Hong Kong. James gathered that it had been organised by the Jockey Club and she had everyone laughing at the scrupulous good manners of the Chinese. No one seemed to be enjoying themselves more than Archie Duncan and their host, both of whom had apparently also been on the trip.

'Did you take your wife with you?' Lady Bellweather

asked the trainer rather pointedly.

'Unfortunately she couldn't come. It was the girl's half term, so she decided to stay at home and do her maternal duties.'

'You men are so selfish. Why, I would never let my husband go away on his own.'

The expression on Lord Bellweather's face suggested that he would leap at such a chance.

Relish now came in and announced that coffee was being served for the ladies in the drawing room.

'Good,' said Sir Randolph. 'We'll have some port here and come and join you later.'

James kept largely silent during the men-only session that followed. After what seemed a lifetime they rejoined the ladies and began a heated discussion on the prospects of the Irish horses in the Gold Cup. At one o'clock James followed the others wearily to bed, a good deal the worse for drink.

It was still very dark outside when he woke up. His dry throat was the penalty for too much champagne and claret, and in addition to a glass of water he desperately needed to relieve his aching bladder. He had never discovered where the bathroom was on his floor, and for a moment he longingly eyed the wash-basin in the corner of his room. But the sound would probably give him away and in any event it didn't solve the problem of a glass for the water. Knowing his luck, Relish would probably jump out of the cupboard when he was in full flow, and instead of shouting 'Caught you, sir!' ask earnestly whether he wanted Earl Grey or Indian tea for breakfast. He decided to go down the corridor and hope that he would come across an open door leading to a bathroom.

Coming out of his bedroom, he turned right and began tiptoeing in the darkness along what seemed acres of plush carpet. He chose not to turn on a light for fear of waking anyone up, although the loud snoring coming from somewhere in the distance suggested that his concern was probably unnecessary. Turning the corner of the corridor, he could see a glimmer of light filtering through from below the door of one of the rooms on his left. Presumably it was a bedroom, and its owner was having a similar problem, but with the advantage of a bathroom en suite. As he crept past, James heard what he thought was a woman's voice followed by groans, which, unless his ear and memory deceived him, were plainly of pleasure. He paused to listen again and this time he was sure that he could also hear a man's voice.

Light playing through the keyhole told him that the key was missing, and he felt a sudden urge to peep through it and see what was going on. His better instinct, the product of a thoroughly decent upbringing, told him to walk on. Sinking to one knee he could make out straight ahead of him a high mahogany bed, its head against the far wall. It reminded him of those Empire beds found in old French hotels. Sitting, or so it seemed, with her naked back to him, was a woman, but the base of the bed itself was over two feet high and partly obscured his view. She was rocking gently back and forth and by her breathing evidently enjoying herself.

James looked round anxiously in case the ghostly figure of Relish should suddenly appear. The Humphrey Bogart line would somehow seem rather out of place this time. But there was no other sound to be heard and James returned to his keyhole. Strain as he might, the man's face was never quite visible. All he could see of him was a pair of hands, one on each of the woman's shoulder blades, guiding her in her movements. The only clue to his identity was the gold ring on his left hand. As to the woman, that was simple. No one else had long black hair like Clarissa Croft.

Chapter 14

The Christie's Foxhunter Chase was run at a furious gallop and James's horse had great difficulty in keeping up with the pace. Fortunately, most of the rest of the field ran out of steam on the second circuit, and James was able to overtake several very tired horses on the run-in to finish what he felt was a very creditable fifth.

The owner-trainer from Somerset did not share his enthusiasm. 'What the 'ell did you think you were doin', Thackeray, droppin' 'im out like that? Did'n' I tell you to keep 'im up with the leaders from the start?'

By now James had dismounted and was anxious to go and weigh in. 'I'm sorry sir, but they just galloped him off his toes with that early pace. He only just got back into the race when the others came back to him.'

'Nonsense! You amateurs are all the same. Can't

judge pace. You ought to stick to writing, young man.'

James could say nothing so he made his way to the weighing room beside the paddock and joined his fellow jockeys in an exchange of hard-luck stories.

Gail, who had come down from London to see him ride, was waiting for him when he had finished changing. She had overhead the comments of the trainer and now delighted in mimicking his West Country accent. 'Aye, that's right, Tack'ry, you never could ride nor write a finish!' she drawled at him.

They walked over to the members' enclosure and fought their way through the throng of Irishmen in the Arkle Bar. Over a bottle of champagne, James told Gail what he had seen during the night. She pretended to be deeply shocked by his behaviour. 'There's a word for people like you!'

'Investigative journalist?' suggested James.

'No. Pervert! Did you see who the man was?'

'No, I told you. All I could see were his hands and what looked like a signet ring.'

'Didn't you look at breakfast to see who was wearing the ring?'

'I didn't have a chance. I had to leave early to come and have a sauna. When I left the house, only Archie was up, and he was in the bathroom.'

'That means you'll never find out − unless of course you bring it up in your next conversation with your employer. "Excuse me, sir". "Yes, Thackeray, what is it, can't you see I'm busy?" "Sorry, sir, I just wondered if I might have a look at your left hand?" "Oh really? And why's that, may I ask?" "I just wanted to see whether you were the man I saw through the keyhole at Raleighs pleasuring Lady Croft." '

James, controlling his laughter, told Gail to keep her voice down. By now, the bar was beginning to empty as the runners for the Gold Cup paraded in front of the stands, and they decided to go and watch the race from the standing area by the rails. James had napped the Irish-trained second favourite and in a desperately tight finish it just beat Archie Duncan's runner. That clearly showed that his horses were in form, and now the National was only three weeks away ... a good omen for The Sportsman.

'I've got to go and interview the winning trainer. I'll meet you in ten minutes or so outside the press room.'

'Fine.'

'There's a boy selling papers over there. Buy me one with tomorrow's runners at Lingfield, would you? I'll do my selections now. Then I can phone the paper with my copy, and we'll be free to stop and have dinner in Oxford on the way home. Does that appeal?'

'Sounds lovely!'

'Good. Then I can tell you all about Lady Bellweather, and the golden years of 1973 to 1986 ... !'

Returning from his interview he found Gail waiting for him with a worried expression. 'I think you'd better read this,' she said, pointing to an item in the stop press section of the back page of the paper.

It read:

DEAD BODY IDENTIFIED

The body of a man found dead in a ditch beside the East Hendred to Wantage road has been identified as Paddy Develera, 35, a stable lad. Police enquires are continuing, pending a post mortem.

'Paddy, the poor bastard.'

'I *am* sorry, James.'

'It doesn't say how long he's been there or how he died or anything. Look, I'm going to give Pale a ring. This all sounds bloody suspicious to me. If Paddy did see something, then I bet he's been got rid of.'

'James, don't you think you ought to be a little careful? I mean, peeping through keyholes is one thing, but let's be realistic, if they thought that Paddy knew something they might also suspect you. I really think you should keep out of this now.'

James looked at her and realised that logically she was right. But like it or not, he was now involved, and the thought of Paddy lying dead in a ditch for so many months made him seethe with anger.

'OK, just let me talk to Pale. If he tells me to mind my own business, I'll do just that.'

'And if not?' Gail's voice was strained.

'If not, we'll just have to see.'

The telephones in the press room were all in use and James had to wait twenty minutes to use one of the public telephones outside the members' stands. Chief Superintendent Pale was expecting his call.

'He was found yesterday by a man walking his dog. In a ditch, beside the road. It looks like he had been hit by a car while riding his bike, but the forensic boys and the pathologist are still working on it.'

'Do you know when it happened?'

'Nobody will say for certain at the moment. The pathologist likes to take his time, and I'm not going to rush him. The problem is that the foxes have got at him and that, plus, the cold weather hasn't made him a very pretty sight. His neck was broken and the abrasions to his chest support the hit-and-run theory.'

'Murder?'

'Careful, young man. Am I talking to Thackeray the journalist, or Paddy's friend, or an amateur sleuth?'

'All three.'

'Fine, then there's no more I'm going to discuss with you on the telephone. Come and see me tomorrow here at the Yard. I am expecting a visit from an old friend of yours and I'm beginning to think that the time has now arrived for you and that newspaper of yours to be of assistance to us.'

'May I ask what?'

'Why not wait and see? Tomorrow, eleven o'clock!'

James's 'old friend' turned out to be Inspector Hardcastle, and judging by the pile of papers and exhibits on Pale's desk the pair had been discussing the Croft case in some detail. The Chief Superintendent beckoned James to sit down and told him that Inspector Hardcastle had some news for him.

'Yes indeed. I understand from my colleague here that you have been expressing some doubts about the guilt of Mr Weatherby. Well, I admit I have all along shared your concern, and during the last month I instructed my officers to make door-to-door enquiries in the area just in case – and I confess I regarded it as a long shot – we found someone who remembered seeing Weatherby wandering around the racecourse at the time the murder was committed. Well, last week we had a bit of luck when a local woman identified him from a photograph as a man she had seen at the races. How can she be so certain, you're wondering? She says she was rushing to watch the first race when she bumped into a man who looked like Weatherby. She remembers him because having knocked her over he proceeded to swear at her and didn't even offer to help her up from the ground.'

'But why has she taken so long to come forward?'

'She says she never reads the papers, and having talked to her I can believe it. Anyway, she's certain enough to have picked him out in an identification parade.'

Pale now intervened. 'This means that the murder hunt is about to be officially reopened, and as you can imagine we are pursuing several lines of enquiry. As we see it – and I think I speak for both of us – there are two possibilities. The first, and the one I prefer, is that Croft was murdered by blackmailers when he refused to meet their demands. The presence of the threatening letter on his body plainly adds weight to that theory. That raises the question how they obtained their information. The answer to that seems to be, by bugging the telephones of well-known trainers, and for all we know, owners and jockeys as well.'

'Did you say trainers in the plural?'

'I did. We checked Croft's phone for a bug but there was nothing in his London flat or his country place. We then checked Archie Duncan's place last week and lo and behold we found a bug in the office in his house.'

'You mean his conversations have also been taped?'

'It looks like it, but he says he has not received any blackmailing threats. Of course the additional advantage of bugging is that the eavesdroppers can use the information to back horses.'

'Or not back them,' James interjected.

'Or not back them, as you rightly point out. That would probably explain the selections on the betting slip which was found on the floor of the horsebox. From what you've already told us, it must have belonged to someone who had access to confidential information.'

'That's right. A shrewd punter might have picked out Marsh's two runners and even Paradise Lost, if he'd watched the horse run at Huntingdon and done his homework on the way he was ridden and the fact that the distance was further than he likes. But there is no earthly reason why he should have picked out Archimedes. His form was terrible and the presence of old Willie Angell on his back suggests to me that he had pulled it on his previous races. I suspect that Duncan was as much in the dark as the rest of us.'

'Good. That brings us then to whether there is any connection between your stable lad's death and Sir Denby's murder.'

'Do you have any more details about Paddy?'

Pale gave him a long hard look. 'You are, if I may say so, a very impatient young man. This is not like a newspaper office with everyone rushing round to obtain exclusives. The pathologist and the forensic boys need time. The latest I heard is that they reckon that the body was in the ditch from before Christmas and they're pretty certain that he was stuck by a car. Given time, they'll probably be able to tell us the make and colour, if not the kind of tyre.'

'Sorry. But have you checked to see whether Angell's car had any dents in it or whether it's recently been to the garage for any repairs?'

Pale shook his head in disbelief. 'We weren't born yesterday. The answer is yes we have, and no it hasn't. We had another session last night with Mr and Mrs Angell and they can't be broken on their alibi. They can even tell us what was on the television the night Paddy disappeared.'

'What's his excuse for telephoning Paddy then?'

'Says simply it wasn't him. Claims he's never heard of the chap and that it's not his habit to socialise with stable lads, particularly Irish ones. One other thing, he doesn't seem to like you very much. He made some uncomplimentary remarks about you poking your nose into other people's business.'

James reacted indignantly. 'I hope you stood up for me.'

'I didn't, actually. Just said I agreed. I don't think it's a good idea for Angell to think you're one of our bloodhounds.'

'Thanks. Presumably you're checking all the local

garages for cars which have come in for repairs to their wings?'

It was now Inspector Hardcastle's turn to lose his patience. 'We are, but I don't think you realise how many garages there are in Berkshire and Oxfordshire alone, and that's not counting how many thousands of cars have been in for repairs in the last few months. If you extend the list to hire cars and make the search nationwide it will take a lot of hard police work and even then some luck on top. It's not like in the books or on TV you know.' He sighed. 'If only it were that simple.'

'I'm sorry. It's just that I blame myself for Paddy's death. When he threw in the remark about what he saw that day I really didn't take him seriously. I thought he was either kidding or just playing at being a secret agent.'

Pale plainly had no time for James's conscience. 'It's our view that he did see the man or possibly men who killed Sir Denby and that he tried a little blackmail himself with fatal results. These people are clearly professional and determined and intimately involved with the racing scene. And this, laddie, is where you come in.'

'What do you mean?'

'The way I see it is that someone out there, Willie Angell or his wife, or even a friend of Paddy, knows something and is afraid to talk or maybe needs some money to loosen his tongue. There is an even better chance of somebody coming forward if we can drop some pretty strong hints that we are on to something.'

'But I can't see where I fit in.'

'Patience. It strikes us that your paper is read by all the people involved in the racing world. Our proposal is simple. We are prepared to let you be the first to break the news of Weatherby's release and of the existence of the betting slip and the possibility of a link between Paddy's death and Denby's murder if you ... ' James caught his breath as Pale paused for maximum effect before continuing, 'persuade the owners of the paper to offer a large reward for information leading to the arrest and conviction of Croft's murderer and the end of this blackmailing racket. Just think what a story it would make – you get an exclusive and all the credit if we nab the villain, and we put a few very nasty and dangerous criminals behind bars.'

'And what if they won't agree? I'm just a humble tipster, you know.'

'You'll have to persuade them. To be blunt, Thackeray, so far you haven't been as helpful as you could have been. Firstly you fail to report to the Inspector here what Paddy told you about seeing those people, and secondly you go off and upset Willie Angell without a word to me about the alleged telephone call he made to Paddy the night before he disappeared. What kind of assistance is that to the police in their enquiries?'

'Okay, okay,' replied James impatiently. 'I've got the message. I warn you now they're a fairly mean lot on the paper and the prospect of offering a reward will not be well received. When would you like the story published?'

'Next Wednesday will be fine. By then we should have a bit more information on Paddy's death, and that's the day the Director of Public Prosecutions is going to announce officially that the charge against Weatherby has been dropped. Good.' Pale rubbed his hands in satisfaction. 'Unless you've any further observations on how we should run the police force?'

'There's just one thing.'

Pale walked around the desk and sat on the edge, looking quizzically into James's face. The young man could understand why that Mitcham gang had caved in, machete or no machete. 'Get it out, lad. I haven't got all day.'

'You said there were two possibilities. But you never mentioned the second.'

'Didn't I? How remiss of me. The second theory is that Croft's murder has nothing to do with blackmail and that the threatening letter was merely a device to lure him to his death and put us on the wrong track. That's where Weatherby originally fitted the bill. But apart from him we can't think of anyone else with a grudge against the man or at least of anyone who wanted him out of the way. Now is that all, Thackeray? Haven't you any racetrack to go to?'

'Thanks. Yes, I have. But one more question – please.' Pale looked to the heavens. 'I forgot to ask it before and it's probably unimportant. But to whom did Weatherby deliver the horse from his yard on the day of the murder?'

'I can answer that,' said Hardcastle. 'It was handed over to its new trainer Archie Duncan, who had been told to collect it by its new owner.'

'And who was that?' enquired James.

'I would have thought you'd know that. Your boss, Sir Randolph Vane.'

Chapter 15

Carlton was a good deal more receptive than Gail to Pale's idea of an article. Over the weekend she had begged James to abandon his role as a sleuth and to realise that Paddy's death meant that they were dealing with hardened criminals, to whom murder was probably nothing more than a domestic chore. All he could reply was that he now owed it to Paddy to see it through, and in any event there was no reason to think he was likely to be the next victim.

Carlton was less keen on the idea of a reward. The paper had not been enjoying a profitable period and he was sceptical about the proprietor going along with the idea.

'But there's nothing to lose,' pleaded James. 'We only have to pay up if the information leads to an arrest and conviction, and if that happens, think of all the publicity – "Newspaper of the Year", a big lunch at The Savoy, glowing tributes to British justice.'

'Give over,' replied Carlton. 'All this talk about justice makes me uneasy. My only concern is whether it will sell newspapers and my instinct is that it probably will. Mark you, we need to produce one or two leads out of it. If I go and sell this upstairs and then we don't receive a single tip, it's your number and not mine that will be in the frame.'

'And if it comes off?'

Carlton mustered a smile. 'Then naturally, as editor, I must accept the credit.'

'Terrific. Can I telephone Pale and tell him that you've given the go ahead?'

'Slow down. I've first got to clear it with you know who, and that may not be so simple. Apart from the money angle he may not want to upset his chums in the Jockey Club. All this blackmail talk gives racing a bad name.'

'You know about that, do you?'

'Know about what? I hate talking in riddles.'

'Sir Randolph being a friend of the Crofts. Lady Croft was staying at Raleighs last week.' James did not add that they seemed to be more than just good friends.

'I only found out that he knew old Croft after the murder. He had me in on the Monday after we published your piece and told me to be very sensitive about the way we treated the story in future.'

'Does he often do that?'

'That's not really your business, but the answer is no. He said merely that the Crofts were good friends of his and he did not want us publishing anything which might upset the grieving widow, or words to that effect.'

'I suppose that's understandable. But you would

have thought he wanted the murderer caught.'

'Who said he didn't? As for her ladyship being a guest at Raleighs, no, I didn't know, almost certainly because you were occupying my bedroom. Now go away and start writing this article for next Wednesday. To add weight, it had better carry both our names. That way I can also win the prize for best investigative journalist!'

As James left the room he overheard Carlton telling his secretary to arrange an immediate meeting with Sir Randolph.

Returning to his desk, James could not resist filling Eric Soper in on all the latest developments. Eric was in high spirits. He had gone through the card at Wimbledon on Saturday night with his selections, and with a 50p accumulator bet he had won over five hundred pounds. He was now planning to blow it all on a weekend with his wife in Paris over Easter. He was very amused to hear of James's stay at Raleighs and the young journalist-cum-Peeping Tom could not resist describing what he had seen through the keyhole.

'I'm convinced it was old Randy I saw.'

'It's right up his street, recently widowed or not. But I thought you said he was all over this Peruvian bird over dinner. The dirty beast.'

'That wouldn't stop him. A bird in the hand followed by one in the bed. And Clarissa Croft, for her age, is no mean looker.'

Eric pretended to look downcast. 'Some men have all the luck.'

'Cheer up. At least you have all your own hair. Randy's must be a wig.'

'A hair weave, to be precise. It has all been kept very quiet but it was done in some clinic in Switzerland, according to my chum on the *Mail*.'

'And ... ?'

But before James could discover any more intimate details about his employer he was summoned in to see Carlton.

'It's not looking too good, I'm afraid. I briefly filled Sir Randolph in on the details, but he was not enthusiastic. He didn't seem at all pleased to hear that Weatherby was going to be released and muttered something about telephoning Lady Croft straight away. He's probably on to her now. I tried to convince him it could only be good for circulation and that it would be a feather in the paper's cap if it led to the arrest of the killer.'

'What about the money?'

'Funnily enough, that did not seem to worry him. Hold on a minute.' The internal telephone rang on his desk.

The manner in which his back subconsciously straightened showed that Carlton was being called by his employer. 'Yes, he's here with me at the moment. I'll send him up at once.'

The editor turned to James. 'He wants to see you now, on the fourth floor. Either he's going to give you the sack or a huge pay increase for investigative journalism, but *I* can't tell you which.'

Sir Randolph's office was spacious and plush. He sat behind a massive, ornate partner's desk covered with telephones, every inch a tycoon.

'All right, Thackeray. What's all this Carlton tells me about the Croft case? He says the police told you they are working on two theories and now want our help in flushing out the villains.'

'Yes, sir, that's roughly it. Chief Superintendent Pale believes it's all the work of blackmailers and tied in with those tapes we received in the Marsh libel case. Alternatively, it could be that Sir Denby was murdered by someone who nursed a sense of grievance or even ...

131

' James paused in anticipation of his employer's reaction, ' ... by someone who knew him and wanted him removed for personal reasons.'

James thought he detected a slight flush rising to Sir Randolph's cheeks but if so, the reaction was momentary.

'Since talking to the editor, I have spoken to Lady Croft who, as you know, is a friend of mine.' (He can say that again, thought James). 'And she was naturally shocked to hear of Weatherby's release. I am most anxious to protect her from prolonged distress over this terrible matter.'

James nodded, seeking to give the impression of being understanding, while at the same time trying, unsuccessfully, to get a look at his employer's left hand, which was firmly ensconced in his jacket pocket.

'If the police feel that this paper can help, and indeed bring these blackmailers to justice, then those are powerful reasons for giving our full cooperation. For my own part, I think it would be far more sensible to concentrate on Pale's first theory than on this nonsense about the killer knowing Sir Denby. Most unlikely.' He got up to show James to the door. 'Good. Then I leave it to you, Thackeray, to reflect my wishes in this article.'

Those wishes, James was well aware, were in fact the proprietor's orders. 'Thank you, sir,' he said, and for the first time saw the gold signet ring which adorned the little finger of his boss's right hand.

In the course of Tuesday, James entered Carlton's office several times with different drafts of the article. The editor was determined to get the tone exactly right and in order, as he put it, to 'hot it up' a bit, decided to give the impression that James might know a little more than he was letting on.

The resulting joint effort was blazoned across the

front page the following morning:

CROFT MURDER SENSATION:
WE OFFER £10,000 REWARD
BY CARLTON WILLIAMS AND
JAMES THACKERAY
EXCLUSIVE

A fresh hunt for the brutal killer of Sir Denby Croft begins today with the announcement by the Director of Public Prosecutions that the charge of murder against northern trainer George Weatherby has been dropped.

Weatherby was arrested last December shortly after the 53-year-old Senior Steward's body was discovered by *Sportsman* journalist James Thackeray in his horse box at Newbury races.

The dead man had been stabbed, the knife piercing the new racing colours he was carrying and fixing them to his corpse. Informed sources at Scotland Yard say that a woman has now come forward and provided an alibi for the accused.

The *Sportsman* is determined that the true assailants shall be brought to justice, and is offering a £10,000 reward for information which effectively leads to their arrest and conviction. This offer has been welcomed by Scotland Yard who are now working on a new theory. *They believe it was the work of blackmailers who have been bugging the phones of trainers and leading owners and jockeys.*

They also believe that the recent death of an Irish stable lad, Paddy Develera, may be connected to Sir Denby's murder and are studying the lad's movements on the night of his disappearance when he arranged to meet a well-known National Hunt jockey.

The *Sportsman* is also able to reveal that their own enquiries, led by James Thackeray, have unearthed certain 'coincidences' about the selections on a betting slip found near Sir Denby's body and thought to have been dropped by his killers.

IF YOU HAVE ANY INFORMATION WHICH MIGHT POSSIBLY HELP DO NOT HESITATE TO CONTACT THE *SPORTSMAN* OFFICES.

Chapter 16

There had been no response to that morning's article in the *Sportsman*, except for a number of calls from clairvoyants offering their services, or 'powers' as they called them, and at 6.30 having written his column and compiled his tips for the following day's three race meetings, James decided that there was no point in hanging around. He recognised that Sir Denby's death had not caused widespread wailing and gnashing of teeth. There is a price to be paid for treating other people like dirt, even if that price is posthumous. But he had hoped that the *Sportsman*'s reward would turn reticence into greed and might have tempted someone to come forward, and in particular that it might have lured Willie Angell into breaking his silence.

As James made for the lift, he passed Eric Soper in

the corridor. That genial operator was on his way back from the staff canteen, the last fragments of a toasted cheese sandwich still in his mouth and on his fingers. Pausing only to wonder out loud whether 'chef' bothered to remove the thin cellophane wrapping before toasting, he wished James good night. It would be at least three hours before all the results of the evening's greyhound races from Harringay were finally through, and he had other chores to do as well. He made his way back to the office feeling bored.

As he walked past James's desk, the telephone rang. Eric picked it up, intending to tell Eileen, the switchboard operator, that James had gone home, but the impatient girl was too quick for him. She was already putting the caller through.

The voice was female, and softly-spoken. 'Is that James Thackeray? I'm phoning about this morning's article.'

Eric didn't hesitate. He knew that James would never forgive him if he let the caller go. 'Yes, Thackeray here. Do you have some information about Sir Denby?'

'I think I do but it's too difficult to talk on the phone. Can we meet?'

'When?'

'Tonight.'

The woman sounded nervous and arguing with her seemed unwise. Eric would have to see if someone else would do the greyhound results. This was his chance for glory and he wasn't going to miss it. 'Where?' he asked.

'Can you be at Fulham Broadway tube station at 9.15? Try not to be late. I'll be on the eastbound platform near the kiosk, about ten yards from the end of the platform.'

'How will I recognise you?'

'I'll be wearing a dark blue coat and a blue and white scarf. And you?'

Eric looked up towards the door where his own coat

was hanging. Beside it he saw the old long brown tweed coat which James always wore to the races but occasionally left in the office, when, like tonight, someone had offered him a lift home.

'I'll be wearing a long dark brown tweed coat and a brown trilby. I'll see you there.'

Eric put down the phone and lit a cigarette. Perhaps he ought to phone James. After all, they could go together. But what if it was all a red herring? Why ruin James's evening? He walked over to Alan Dobson, the horse racing results sub-editor, who was reading a copy of the evening paper by his desk in the corner of the room.

'Alan, mate. Can you do me a favour?'

'Depends what it is and how much it's going to cost me.'

'A bit of an emergency at home. My youngest's not too well. Could you do the greyhound results? I'll have to leave by 8.30 but you should be able to get away easily before ten.'

'It's a bit difficult. I promised the missus we'd go to the cinema. Still, you helped me out last week, so suppose I'll have to risk her wrath. She's pretty understanding about these things on the whole.'

'You're a pal. I won't forget it.'

'Think nothing of it, old lad.'

Alan reached for the phone to give his wife the bad news, and Eric moved off to his desk.

At 8.30 exactly Eric left the *Sportsman* building and took the District Line train from Blackfriars to Earl's Court. There he changed and waited for a Wimbledon train. He was beginning to have second thoughts about this exploit, but it was now too late to phone James. At 9.08 the train arrived and within about three minutes it was pulling into Fulham Broadway station.

Eric looked up from his newspaper and gasped. The whole platform space on both sides of the track was jam-packed with people – men, young boys, the occasional woman, half of them wearing blue and white scarves, the other half red and white ones. Jesus, a football crowd! Eric belatedly remembered that Chelsea had been playing at home that evening to Arsenal in a London derby. The tube doors opened and the crowd surged in, shouting and screaming the names of the opposing teams. Pushing, shoving and using his elbows, Eric forced his way out of the carriage, and with almost equal difficulty up to the top of the stairs and across the bridge which led down to the eastbound platform.

The same chaos reigned there as Eric slowly worked his way past the menacing looking youths, the anxious fathers clutching young children, the middle-aged drunks, the girls laughing hysterically as they swayed on their boyfriends' arms, towards the end of the platform and the appointed rendezvous. He could see no sign of a lady in a dark blue coat and blue and white scarf but it was almost impossible to be certain. He continued to look around, but with an increasing feeling that he had been hoaxed.

He was facing the line when he felt the shove in his back. Its force carried him past the passengers on the edge of the platform looking to their right at the oncoming train. His arms flailed the air as he sought for something to hang on to – a coat sleeve, a scarf, anything.

His head hit the electric rail just as the front cabin of the frantically breaking train tore into his body. In a second he had disappeared from view, his final scream drowned in the nightmare chants of 'Chelsea! Chelsea!' 'Arsenal! Arsenal!'

Chapter 17

The ring of the doorbell of James's flat took Gail by
surprise. She had come over from her own flat and
found him extremely depressed by the lack of response
to the article. As she had pointed out, it was hardly
likely that someone was going to telephone in and
confess, while any informer would take time to find the
courage to come forward and if it was to be someone
like Willie Angell's wife the price had to be right. These
sensible words had had little or no effect. James had
wandered around the flat with a long face waiting for
the telephone to ring with a call re-routed from the
office. By eight-thirty she could bear it no longer and
ordered him off to the A.B.C. cinema in the Fulham
Road to catch the late performance of the Woody Allen
film. She herself stayed behind to prepare a roughage-
free meal as a treat.

It was now only 10.15 and she flung open the door expecting to see a self-pitying face and to hear some tale about how the man in the next seat in a dirty raincoat kept on giving him strange looks. James was convinced that queers lurked in every corner.

The sight of two uniformed policemen took her by surprise. 'Oh, I'm sorry. I thought you were somebody else,' she exclaimed.

The elder of the two, a sergeant with a kindly face which reminded her of her father, took off his helmet and asked very politely whether this was Mr James Thackeray's flat, and if so, could they come in.

'Yes, this is James's flat, but he's not here at the moment. He's gone to the cinema. I'm not expecting him back till after eleven. Is there anything I can do or do you want to come back later?'

There was a certain sombreness about their expressions which made her feel uneasy.

'There's nothing wrong, is there?' Her voice became uncertain as she led them into the sitting room.

The younger officer, no more than a boy, looked sheepishly at the sergeant. 'I'm sorry to ask you this, miss,' he said, 'but are you a relation or close friend of Mr Thackeray?'

'There *is* something wrong, isn't there?' She looked at the pained expressions on their faces. 'I suppose you would call me his girlfriend.' She cursed herself for having played so hard to get. 'What's happened? Tell me, for God's sake.'

The sergeant moved forward to put his arm round her shoulder while the younger policeman played nervously with his helmet and looked round the room. 'I'm afraid there's been a terrible accident. About an hour ago a man fell in front of a tube train at Fulham Broadway and we have reason to believe it was Mr Thackeray.'

Gail stared at him in disbelief. 'But it can't be!' By now her voice was becoming hysterical. 'He's gone to the cinema, I tell you. There must be some terrible mistake.'

'What time would that have been, miss? Don't you think you would be better sitting down?'

'I'm perfectly all right standing up,' she snapped. She realised that she was losing control and willed herself to be strong. 'I'm sorry, officer. It's just that I can't believe it could be James.'

'I quite understand. This is a terrible shock. Now, when did you say he went off?'

'About 8.30, or at the latest 8.45. I was in the kitchen. It's only a few minutes' walk to the cinema and the performances don't start till nine. I just don't believe it's him. What proof do you have?'

'From what we've been told' – here the sergeant took out a note book and referred to it – 'the dead man was wearing a tweed overcoat. Inside one of the pockets were found two opened letters addressed to Mr Thackeray at this address and a diary with the initials J.O.T. Oh yes, and inside the diary was a credit card in his name. I'm sorry to have to ask you this, but was he wearing a coat of that description when he left tonight?'

'I don't know, but I'm sure I saw that coat in the hall when I answered the door.' She rushed into the hall, willing it to be on its normal peg.

'It's gone!' she cried, and returned to the room in tears. 'I know, he's been mugged on his way to the cinema and whoever stole his coat fell in front of the train.'

The officers' faces made her realise how much she was clutching at straws.

'It will be necessary to have an identification. Do you know where we can contact his next of kin?'

'His mother, she's a widow and lives in Dorset. But can't she be spared that ordeal? She loved him so much.'

The sergeant had picked up a photograph of James on a beach in Bermuda shorts, grinning inanely at the camera.

'Is this him?'

Gail nodded. 'Yes. It was taken last summer before we met. He used to say those shorts drove all the girls wild.'

'Perhaps you would feel better identifying him in the morning, miss. You might be a little stronger by then.'

'No, we must go now. I'll fetch my coat.'

'I must warn you that he won't be a very pretty sight. If it's any consolation, he would have died instantly on hitting the live rail.'

Gail stifled her tears as she accompanied the policemen to the hospital, which was only a few streets away. The casualty ward bore vivid testimony to the rivalry between the respective football fans and their injuries ranged from cuts and bruises to broken noses and slashed faces. Only Chief Superintendent Pale would have felt at home at the sight of one still-belligerent youth with his right ear lobe hanging off. To add tone to the setting, a drunk was remonstrating with a polite yet determined staff nurse who appeared immune to his foul language.

Gail was taken downstairs to the mortuary, a windowless room in the basement. The sergeant spoke quietly with the gaunt-faced white-haired attendant who then went to open a large refrigerator-like door, set into one of the side walls. He pulled out a stainless steel drawer with an ease which made Gail shudder. Inside was a body enclosed in a shroud. Even the policemen were looking distinctly green as the attendant undid the tapes and almost with a flourish pulled back the hood.

142

He beckoned Gail forward. It was the hardest step she had ever had to take. There was dried blood caked around the left ear, the hair was charred, and the face was just a solid lifeless lump of flesh. It could have been anybody. The attendant, as if in an act of respect, stepped back from the drawer and as he did so Gail caught sight of a blue patch on the left shoulder. The sergeant caught her as she fainted.

She regained consciousness in his arms a few seconds later. 'I'm sorry, love,' he said. 'It must be ghastly for you. Can you recognise him?'

'No. But it's not James.'

'How can you be so sure?'

She was trembling and sobbing. 'Look at his shoulder.'

The sergeant walked reluctantly over to the corpse and slowly and cautiously lifted up the open shroud between his forefinger and thumb.

'What about his shoulder, miss?' he asked Gail in a gentle voice as he peered into the drawer.

Her reply, whispered, was almost inaudible. 'It's not him.' There was a pause in which the stench of the mortuary momentarily dominated their senses. 'You see, James doesn't have a tattoo.'

The sergeant looked down again at the lifeless occupant of the drawer and gulped. He had never seen a tattoo of a greyhound before.

Chapter 18

James sprang from his chair and made towards the front door when he heard the key in the lock. Gail entered, looked at him, flung herself into his arms, and burst into a flood of tears.

James offered a none-too-clean handkerchief. 'Hey, what's up?' he said. 'Where did you go? It's been like the Marie Celeste in here. I was worried.'

Gradually, through her sobs, Gail told him what had happened.

He was frightened as well as puzzled. Who would have wanted to steal his tweed coat, and why? And the tattoo of the greyhound. Eric? But it couldn't be. In a state of growing shock, which made him sound slightly hysterical, he telephoned Carlton Williams at his home.

'Is this some sort of joke? Because if it is, it's in very bad taste.'

'No, it's serious. If it is Eric, what was he doing at the tube station? Everybody knows he hates football.'

'I just hope you're wrong. I'll phone up the front desk and see what time he left. I don't want to go frightening his missus unnecessarily. I'll call you back.'

He did so, almost at once.

'It looks bad,' he said. 'The commissionaire says he saw him leave at 8.30, but was surprised because he didn't say his usual goodnight or pass on his tip for next day. I've tried to get hold of Alan on the results desk but he's not home yet. His wife says that he telephoned earlier to say he was staying on late at the office to help Eric out, as one of his kids was ill. Did you know anything about that?'

'He never mentioned it to me. Do you know if Eric had a tattoo?'

'That's not the kind of thing I normally ask my staff. However, I'm afraid it's possible. Don't forget, Eric did his National Service in the navy.'

'Are you going to phone his home?'

'It now looks like I've got to. He won't be best pleased with me if I put him in it with his wife when all he's done is go out for a bit of fun on the town.'

'Eric? He loves his family.'

'Thanks for making it so easy for me. However, you can keep your fingers crossed while I phone poor Jane.'

After what seemed an age but was in fact just a few minutes, the phone rang again.

'Bad news. He's not back, the children are fine and – here's the shaker – he did have a tattoo. Done when he was in the navy and regretted ever since.'

'What did you tell her?'

'That we thought he had been involved in an accident and I was coming down straight away to see her. Do you think you can alert the police?'

'Of course.'

145

'And James, one last thought. Are the police sure it was an accident?'

'What do you mean?'

'Because if it wasn't, the real victim was meant to be you.'

The news of the tragedy was greeted with incredulity and grief at the paper's offices. With his kindness and sense of humour, his gift for listening to other people's problems, and his entertaining interpretations of the schemes and privates lives of the management, Eric had been extremely popular throughout the building, from the editorial floor to the secretaries and the canteen staff. It was agreed he would be irreplaceable.

Rumours began to spread as to what had really happened that night. Although the offical line was that a ghastly accident had taken place, everyone knew of their late colleague's feelings towards 'Oikball' as he called it.

Plainly his excuse of leaving early to go home was a pretence. But what for, and why? He wasn't a serious gambler, and he didn't have a girl on the side. The obvious answer was that the Croft article must have something to do with it, and from this it was only a step to putting the blame for the tragedy on James.

Some of the older journalists welcomed the opportunity to have a go at the new boy, who, they felt, had got too big for his boots. Almost everyone went about saying that if he hadn't got involved in the murder case, Eric would still be alive. Bitter silence replaced the banter when James came into the room. It was a painful and unpleasant period.

James could not blame his colleagues. He, too, had been fond of Eric and he knew full well that the wrong man had been lured to his death. Carlton tried to pretend that the death had been accidental and even

Pale refused to commit himself. Cautiously, he thought of offering James round-the-clock surveillance but soon accepted that this would be unrealistic – unless he could find a plain-clothes detective who also had a jockey's licence.

In any case, the police enquiries as to what had happened that night were proving unfruitful. Eileen, the scatter-brained telephonist, was no help. She could not remember putting any calls through to Eric at the time in question, nor could she say whether anyone had tried to ring James. And she certainly could not recall whether the caller, if there had been one, had been a man or a woman. 'I'm on my own in the evening,' she wailed. 'I can't remember everything. I wish I could. Poor Mr Soper.'

James sat at home during the next two evenings, planning what he should do next. He could well be a marked man, but that only made him more determined to see through to the end the hunt for the killers of Croft, Paddy, and now Eric.

Now and again he gave way to self-pity, asking plaintively, 'Why couldn't it have been me?' until Gail snapped back, 'I just thank God every day it wasn't. And if you were honest with yourself you'd do the same. I liked Eric, sure, and so did you. But I'm still glad it's you who's alive.' And she stormed out of the room.

'Look,' she said later, 'I won't ask you to give this business up because you won't and you'd only lie to me. All I beg of you is to be careful. The National is next week and so many people are counting on you. Promise me to do nothing more until after it's over and then I'll help you. Please?'

James agreed. He only hoped that whoever out there was stalking him would also be prepared to wait.

Chapter 19

It had been arranged that the box taking The Sportsman would leave Archie Duncan's yard on Thursday morning, to give the horse a day to recover from its journey before Saturday's race. Carlton was determined to extract as much free publicity as possible from the occasion and in addition to a posse of Fleet Street photographers had even persuaded the BBC to send down a film unit. James and the lucky new owner were asked to pose in a variety of adoring positions near the horse and he winced at the jibes he would receive from his friends when they saw it on the television preview before the race. Archie was in a confident and enthusiastic mood and actually made some very complimentary comments about James's ability as a jockey.

By mid morning the press had taken their share of film and having waved goodbye to the horsebox James and Gail were ready to set off. They had a trip of well over two hundred miles ahead and Clare, Archie's elder step-daughter, could not resist poking her usual fun at the battered old Morris. She lent Gail some home-recorded music to while away the tedious hours ahead. 'If you can hear the tapes above the din of the engine,' she added tartly.

They left the M1 near Melton Mowbray and had lunch in a pretty village pub. Both struggled to conceal their anxieties, well knowing that if one gave way both would probably break, and that James would then be emotionally in no fit state to ride on the next two days. The late chance of a ride in the famous amateur's race on the Friday, the Foxhunter's, had ensured that they had something to distract their attention from the graver dangers in the background.

Leaving the pub, James suggested a short diversion to the nearby village of Little Blenerhassett.

'Why's that name so familiar?' Gail asked. 'Don't we know somebody who lives here?'

'Lives is a bit out of date. A certain deceased Senior Steward of the Jockey Club had his house here and I want to make one or two enquiries while we are in the area.'

'Oh really? So it wasn't just a coincidence that you chose that pub for lunch! You promised to abandon your so-called sleuthing until after the National. James Thackeray, you're a liar! There's no other word for it.'

They soon reached the outskirts of the village and James pulled up outside the gates of a large Georgian house.

'We're not going in, are we?' Gail asked nervously.

'No. Just thought I'd have a look. Anyway, I doubt whether Lady Croft is at home. She's almost certainly on her way to Aintree to join old Randy's house party.'

They drove on and stopped at a small garage in the village. According to the sign above the forecourt, Wainright's garage did repairs as well as supplying petrol. The owner was extremely friendly and as he filled up the Morris with petrol he chatted happily away with James.

'Where are you off to?' he asked.

'We're going up to Aintree for the National. I'm a journalist on a racing paper.'

'Lucky bugger, being able to mix business with pleasure!'

'Don't I know it. I may be mistaken, but isn't this where that poor chap Denby Croft used to live, the one who was murdered?'

'That's right. A fine house, and the family have lived there for ages. It's empty most of the time now, though. The second Lady Croft never was very keen on it. They say she prefers city life.'

'I suppose the Crofts were good for business here, what with maintaining their cars and their petrol bills?'

'Not bad, but the old man used to get his Bentley serviced in London by the people who sold it to him. Although we did do a repair job for her ladyship on the car last year before Christmas. Damn good job we did, too.'

Before James could ask any more questions, the phone started ringing in the garage office. 'Excuse me sir, I must go. I'm expecting an important call. That'll be ten pounds, sir.'

James handed over the money and waited for a receipt before returning to the Morris and a rather grumpy Gail.

It was just getting dark when they arrived in Liverpool and began the hunt for a suitable bed-and-breakfast sign. Although the other journalists were staying at the famous Adelphi, James was anxious to avoid the endless parties in an effort to keep his weight down. That at least was what he told Carlton.

But both he and Gail knew that their real intention was to find somewhere quiet and well out of harm's way.

After a good deal of searching they came across a small boarding house outside Southport and only a few miles from the course. Mrs Crow, the landlady, gave them a disapproving glance as she answered the door and grudgingly admitted that she had vacancies. She gave Gail a glare of offended morality as she noted the absence of a wedding ring – and was even more put out when the young couple asked for two rooms, like a priest robbed of a juicy confession. Feeling exhausted, they declined her offer of a lukewarm Lancashire hotpot and collapsed, within range of their hostess's attentive ear, into their separate beds.

They left Mrs Crow's ornate nest the following morning in better spirits than when they had arrived, but it was only when they had turned off the Melling Road and into the car park reserved for owners, trainers and jockeys that James was able to concentrate fully on the prospect of two glorious days' racing ahead. He comforted himself with the thought that if someone out there wanted to kill him they would hardly choose a packed racecourse, where there would be little opportunity to find him on his own. Having parked the old Morris among the glittering array of Bentleys, Jaguars and Range Rovers, James collected his helmet and other kit from the boot and they made their way towards the entrance to the course. Though the sun was shining, the biting north wind still made its presence felt. Happily, however, it had not deterred the numerous picnic parties standing by their cars from eating, drinking and swapping selections for the day's races. James wondered whether any of them had ever sat down and added up the true cost of keeping a horse in training, but then again you cannot measure pleasure in money terms alone. He just thanked God that people didn't, because if they did, he would be out of a job.

He spotted Charlie Catchpole, the owner of Deep Purple, the horse he was to ride in the Foxhunter's, standing with the jockey who would have ridden it but for a skiing accident. They walked over to say hello.

'All keyed up, James? I'm relying on you to win this race for me.'

'I'll do my best not to let you down, Charlie.'

'Good man. How about a drink or a bite to eat?'

James looked enviously at the pile of food and drink stacked in the boot of the Rolls Royce. 'Go on, tuck in,' a voice inside him shouted.

'No thanks, but I'm sure Gail would like some. I'm taking things easy so that tomorrow I'll be light enough to use a decent size saddle, as Archie refuses to believe that I'll be able to do the right weight and I have absolutely no intention of giving him an excuse to jock me off. There are times when I think he'd leap at the chance.'

'No, never. You're quite wrong there. He thinks you're a very good jockey for an amateur, and has even had a bet on the horse.'

'All the more reason not to risk his wrath, then. Do you mind if I leave Gail here with you? I want to walk round the National Course before the race today.'

'Fine. Just make sure you show me sufficient respect in the paddock. We owners can be very difficult, you know!' Charlie roared with laughter at his own remark, and returned to the beckoning hamper.

Chapter 20

Once inside the course, James made his way past the endless hospitality marquees, already filled with laughter and high spirits, and across the wide stretch of tarmac to the old brick and tiled building which housed the Red Rum bar, the Stewards' Room and the jockeys' changing room. Adjoining the front, and equally ancient, was the enclosure reserved for the first three home in each race. James could not resist walking into the largest berth, reserved for the winner, and picturing to himself just what it must be like to be led there as the victorious jockey in the National. Today, an hour before the first race and without the huge jostling crowds, the scene around him looked desolate, with betting slips fluttering in the wind like so much confetti, a vivid reminder of yesterday's disappointments.

He walked into the changing room and handed his bag to the valet.

'How many rides have you got today, Jim?', asked Ernie, well aware in fact that James, as an amateur, very rarely had more than one.

The latter refused to be put down by this touch of Geordie humour. 'I've been offered one in every race, actually', he replied grandly, 'but in view of the National tomorrow I've decided to space myself and only ride in the Foxhunter's.'

'Go on,' said Ernie. 'Really?' His look implied: 'Come off it!'.

'I'm going to walk the course. See you later.'

'Bloody amateur!' muttered the valet, not quite loud enough for James to hear, as he made for the National start, which lay ahead and to the right of the stands.

Soon he had passed under the eighty yards or so of webbing tape which tomorrow would be the starting line. Then, to keep warm, he jogged the two hundred yards to where the much sharper 'Mildmay Course' veered off to the left and parted from the National which carried on straight over the Melling Road. Since only the Foxhunter's would be run over the National fences that afternoon, the huge iron gates which opened up to let the runners through were still locked. James made his way towards the small gate on the right hand side, collected one of the pass-out tickets, and crossed to a similar gate which led to the rest of the racecourse. By the side of the road stood a huge J.C.B. and an enormous pile of black grit. About three quarters of an hour before the Foxhunter's race began, the road would be blocked off and the grit spread across to create a reasonable surface about nine inches deep over which the horses could gallop. The blackness of the grit would be in sharp contrast to the grass which preceded it and it was scarcely surprising that more than one horse had tried to jump the entire road thinking it was a ditch.

The first two fences seemed to be slightly larger than James remembered from his past visits to the course, but that had only been as a spectator. Today and tomorrow he would have to jump them. Like all National fences they were made of dark green spruce, unlike the black birch which was used on most other British racecourses. At the front there was a nice big belly to stop the horses coming too close to the bottom of the fence before take-off. It was strange to think that so many horses fell at these two fences every year. The reason, apparently, or so James had been told, was because they approached them too quickly and were fooled by the slight but unexpected drop on the landing side. At the point where the horse expected to come into contact with the ground it found itself still airborne: then, when it did touch down, it was not ready for the landing, lost balance, and knuckled over. Rather like its backers!

The third fence bore little resemblance to the first two and the butterflies in James's stomach told him to walk by without looking up. Apart from 'The Chair', which came later, and the open ditch at Auteuil in France, which boasts a huge white tree trunk as a guard rail, this fearsome fence had to be the most intimidating in the world. Five feet two inches high, almost four feet across, and with a six-foot ditch in front, there was little room for error. Any horse which had misjudged its stride for take-off and overstepped the guard rail would have a horrible fall. James nervously recalled that the inside of all the fences at Aintree were built round telegraph poles sunk into the ground and not even half a ton of horse travelling at twenty-eight miles an hour would move them. At least, he consoled himself, the top six inches of spruce knocked off quite easily.

He walked quickly past the next two fences which were more or less identical to the first and reached the famous Becher's Brook, set on the apex of a left hand bend and therefore at a much steeper angle. From the take-off side the jump looked relatively simple and one wondered what all the fuss was about. James saw the reason when he walked round to the landing side, and with a sense of doom and disbelief looked up to the top of the fence some five feet above his head. You could almost parachute from there. From where he was standing, on the inside by the running rail, the drop was a good three feet more than it was further along towards the outside and he now decided to keep to that side tomorrow. He would leave it to the smart boys who knew what they were doing and had good jumpers beneath them to jump the fence on an angle on the inside.

He glanced at his watch. He had already taken twenty minutes and was not even half way round. He hurried past the next fence, which was the smallest, but the scene of a famous pile-up in 1967, then on to the Canal Turn. Here he would either have to jump at an angle or slow up considerably so he could land and still have time to turn. He decided to do both. The consequence of failure was the confrontation at a flat-out gallop with the ten-foot high corrugated-iron fence which separated the canal from the racecourse.

By now he was at the part of the course farthest from the stands and he knew that if he was lucky enough still to be in the race at this point tomorrow on the second circuit it would be in the time when the pace started to hot up. He had once been told by a former champion jockey that it was the psychological feeling of turning for home that caused a lot of jockeys to make their move too soon, and he only hoped that in the excitement he would remember to keep cool.

He crossed the Melling Road again, past another waiting J.C.B. and pile of grit, and rejoined the racecourse proper. Walking back to the press room he could not avoid looking at the deadly Chair fence which stood just to the left of the grandstand: five feet ten inches high, six feet across and with a wide ditch in front which looked large enough to float a liner. James put aside his fantasies of coming first. He simply hoped he would be able to jump round safely, and in particular that no harm would befall The Sportsman.

He watched the first race and then went to change for the Foxhunter's which was the third race on the card. He had just finished putting on his lucky muffler, a present from his late father, when the man on the door called out that Mick, Archie's head lad, was waiting for him to weigh out. He quickly put on his riding boots, stood up, and took his saddle from the valet's table. Then he walked round the corner and stood on the big red Avery trial scales, beginning to feel really excited about the race ahead of him. The needle settled at 11st 12lb.

'I need another two pounds,' he shouted out to Ernie. The latter, who was wearing a pair of jeans and a blue apron, now passed him two six-inch square pieces of flat lead almost before he had finished speaking. The needle jumped to the correct weight of 12 stone and after Ernie had put one piece of lead into each side of the weight cloth so as to keep it even, James went into the weighing room to pick up his number cloth. Black cloths today, with white numbers, because the race was being televised. Normally it was the other way around. James could never understand why and nobody he asked knew the reason.

He thumbed his way down the racecard to see what number he was and then picked up the 'seven' and placed it on top of his saddle. He was now ready to weigh out officially and walked across to the other side of the crowded room and sat on the scales.

'Number seven with a breast plate, sir,' he shouted to the Clerk of the Scales.

'Have you shown your medical book, Thackeray?' replied the official.

'No, sir.' Realising his error, James put the saddle down on the table in front of him and hurried back inside to fetch his medical book from his jacket pocket.

When he returned, the Clerk of the Scales was in an awkward mood. 'Don't show it to me, Thackeray. It's the man over there who wants to see it.' He pointed towards a grim-faced figure sitting under a sign which read 'Medical Records'.

Mick, who had been watching this performance from the other side of the rail which divided the weighing room now lent over and shouted to James to 'pull his finger out', as he was running out of time to put the saddle on. The official did not share the lad's sense of urgency and slowly and carefully scrutinised the book to ensure that the last entry was written in blue and not red, thus indicating that James was fit to ride. He gave the young journalist the kind of look you receive from customs men at the Italian border and which induces even in the most law-abiding travellers an almost irresistible urge to confess.

'It's all right, Mr Soames,' he called over to the Clerk of the Scales, and now James was able to weigh out. His weight and breast plate were duly noted in Mr Soames' book.

Mick grabbed the saddle anxiously from him as James asked, 'Has this horse got any chance?'

'Yes, if you don't fall off it,' came the reply.

Mick had never liked him, or so it appeared, subscribing, no doubt, to the school of thought which held that all amateurs are born with silver spoons in their mouths. James wryly reflected that just at the moment, he didn't seem to have many friends.

The second race had just finished and the jockeys were filing back through the weighing room. It had been won by a horse ridden by Richard Sanderson, the champion jockey, and a great cheer went up as the jockeys watched the race on the television set in the far corner of the changing room. James, who had joined them, suddenly felt a dig in his ribs. It was Willie Angell. Mud covered his breeches and he looked as surly and menacing as ever.

'A little bit of advice, Thackeray. Keep your nose and ears out of other people's business. I'd hate to read in the papers one morning that you never got to use your return ticket on the tube.'

James moved away. This was not the moment for a row. One of the officials was shouting 'Jockeys for the next race', the signal that they were to make their way to the paddock.

Normally, most of the amateurs could not get out on the course quick enough, in contrast to the professionals, and they were already clustering round the door. James noticed one rider standing a little apart and looking distinctly uneasy, his goggles already down. If he was silly enough to do that, he was silly enough to do anything, thought James, and made a mental note to remember his colours so as to give him a wide berth. Deciding it would be unkind not to say anything he went over to the lonely figure.

'Hello. I'm James Thackeray,' he said.

'Hi, I'm Tom Tracy.' The young man, who could not have been more than twenty, held out his hand. James noticed that instead of a proper race whip he had only an old pony-club one which he held with his hand through the loop to prevent himself from dropping it. If any of the professionals saw this they would give him a ribbing he wouldn't forget in a hurry.

'Don't mind me saying this, but you needn't pull your goggles down until we're at the start. Otherwise you might look a bit silly.'

Tom thanked him and fumbled with his whip as he tried to pull the goggles back over the peak of his cap.

'Here, let me do it.'

Soon they were following the other jockeys towards the parade ring through the throng of spectators.

'Is this your first ride under rules?' James asked.

'Yes. I've ridden my father's horses in point-to-points and had a go team chasing but this is my first time on a real racecourse.'

'You're throwing yourself in at the deep end a bit, aren't you? Have you walked the course?'

'Crawled it, more like. I got as far as the Chair, nearly fainted and came back.'

'Why are you riding, then?'

'Something called filial duty. My father was a great horseman in his day and he bought this horse I'm riding from a farmer friend of his when he saw it was entered.'

'I suppose it could have been worse. He could have bought one for the National.'

'Thanks! I'm prepared to do it this once, but after that, at the great age of nineteen, I'm going to announce my retirement.'

'What will you do then?'

'It's the quiet life for me. I'm going to train to be a journalist.'

James grinned but said nothing.

Entering the enclosure he made his way over to a group composed of Archie, Charlie and his wife, and Gail. He touched his cap in a show of mock deference, and Charlie, thus encouraged, assumed the role of arrogant owner, barking instructions at his hapless jockey.

The bell rang for the jockeys to mount. The party wished him good luck, then Mick helped him onto the horse and his lad led him round the paddock. His lad was full of optimism about the horse's chances. 'He would win today pulling a cart,' he announced loudly. And although James had never sat on the animal before he liked him the moment he was in the saddle.

Deep Purple had a good strong neck set on to lovely wide shoulders and paraded around with a real sense of purpose. He was the third to leave the Paddock and just before the lad let him go to canter to the start he said something which took James by surprise.

'Come back safely, mate. That's the main thing. Look after the horse, but most of all, look after yourself.'

No lad had ever said that to him before, and as he shortened his reins to canter away his spirits perked up and he hoped that Deep Purple would win – for the lad's sake most of all.

There was quite a long way to the start and he cantered down slowly. Tom and two others passed him out of control and for a moment Deep Purple tried to go with them. James took a tighter hold on the reins. Tom and the others had not had the brains to separate, and so their three horses thought that the race had started. They had gone halfway down to the Canal Turn before they eventually pulled up, causing the start of the race to be delayed.

Once all the girths had been checked, the starter called them into line. Of the twenty runners, fifteen were spread across the tapes, ready to get a flyer. It looked like the beginning of a five furlong race before they introduced starting stalls.

James noticed Tom to the side of him. 'Whereabouts are you going?' he asked.

'I don't know yet.'

'Your goggles aren't down.' James wished he had not

mentioned the fact because as Tom took one hand off the reins the starter let the tapes go and his horse whipped round, leaving him facing the wrong way.

It was a flat-out gallop to the first – which would be the second last in tomorrow's National – and James allowed Deep Purple to run along with the rest until they were about twenty yards away from it. He then checked him back so as to get his hocks underneath his quarters and thus jump as he should. A gap had opened up nicely in front of him to give a good view of the fence and meeting it exactly right for take-off Deep Purple jumped it effortlessly. The horse was so sure of himself that his confidence infected James, who now felt himself really looking forward to the rest of the race.

By the time they reached the second (the last in the National) the field was already quite well strung out. Again Deep Purple met it perfectly and jumped it well. But just as he was about to come down on the other side another horse came up from behind him on his inside and, travelling half as fast again, jumped right across his path. Poor Deep Purple had nowhere to land and crashing into the back legs of the other horse took a horrible fall, throwing James high in the air and catapulting him a good ten feet.

Once he had stopped rolling and was certain that there were no more horses behind him, James looked up and tried to recognise the idiot who had wrecked what looked like being a dream first ride round Aintree. He might have guessed. It was Tom. He had just started cursing him when he realised that something was the matter. Instead of making for the Chair, which was the next fence, Tom was galloping towards the grandstand with his left rein hanging loose from the bit.

He did not wait to see where he ended up as behind him Deep Purple was struggling to get up and the way he was acting made James fear that something was broken. He ran over to him, feeling for the first time the ache in his own backside where he had hit the ground. The horse was on his feet and, to James's enormous relief, seemed all right. He had only once had a horse break a leg with him. It had upset him for days.

By now the racecourse doctor, following in his car, had come to see if he was all right. A brief examination revealed no obvious signs of concussion, although the soreness on his backside suggested that the skin might be badly scraped and need fairly urgent dressing. On the doctor's orders James was shepherded by a St John's Ambulance attendant into a waiting ambulance and driven back to the casualty room behind the weighing room, where it was agreed he would wait until the doctor returned at the end of the race. Feeling decidedly sore, both physically and emotionally, he thought he'd better lie down, choosing the cubicle furthest from the door and the noise. As he collapsed onto the bed, one of the two St John's nurses on duty brought him a cup of tea, while her colleague wheeled in a trolley laden with surgical dressings.

James lay on his front, having removed his muffler and put it on the table beside his tea. Staring at the grey wall in front of him and supporting himself on his right elbow he reflected on his bad luck and the disappointment of Charlie and Mick. At least Tom would not be riding in the National. In the background he could hear the attendants laughing and chatting, as they washed up the cups and saucers.

The sudden flash of leather before his eyes was followed by a relentless band of pressure round his throat. His neck was jerked violently backwards by an unseen force behind him and a knee, planted firmly between his shoulder blades, stopped him moving. He struggled wildly to get his fingers inside the cord, which

163

was now burning his skin. But its tautness, and the strength of his unknown attacker, prevented them from getting a grip. He tried to rise from the couch but his assailant was too strong and well positioned. By now the pain behind his eyes was unbearable, his head felt as if it was about to explode, and all he could see was a warm red glow. In a last desperate and meaningless gesture he kicked out with his legs. All he heard was a metallic crack as the pain ceased and everything went black.

When he came round his throat was aching and throbbing. He tried to swallow but it was like ingesting razor blades. Putting his hand to his throat he could feel the weals around his Adam's apple. The utensils on the trolley were in disarray. James realized that he must have kicked it as he desperately flailed about and that it had been this clatter which had caused his attacker to flee. In his panic whoever it was had dropped on the floor the piece of rein which only a few minutes before was wrapped around James's neck.

Taking the forceps from the trolley, James carefully picked it up and wrapped it in one of the disposal bags beside the medicine tray. His first instinct was to get out as quickly as possible. If the doctor saw the weals on his throat there would be no chance of his being allowed to ride tomorrow; the only certainty would be a red entry in his medical book. Nor did he fancy being interviewed by the local police. That bit must be left to Pale.

Putting on his muffler to hide the weal marks, he tiptoed out of the cubicle and past the room where the nurses were still washing up and listening to the commentary of the fifth race on the local radio. They had obviously not heard the clatter of the trolley above the noise of their chatter and the radio, but his attacker was not to know that. He tried to shout out that he would come and see the doctor before the races

164

tomorrow but he could do no more than mouth the words, such was the agony in his throat. Turning down the passage, he hurried towards the changing room and was about to enter it when he heard Gail calling his name.

'Are you all right? We saw you fall and being put in the ambulance. We were all worried about you.'

He turned round, to see Archie Duncan, Clarissa Croft and Sir Randolph also hovering.

'That was very bad luck, James,' said Archie. 'Lady Croft and Sir Randolph saw what happened from their box and came over to see how you were. I met them here.'

James did his best to answer. 'I'm fine, thank you, sir.' He was determined not to give the trainer a chance to jock him off for the National.

'It was very ...' he paused to catch his breath, '... kind of you all to be so concerned.'

'Are you sure you're all right, James?' It was Gail speaking again.

James's eyes begged her not to ask any more questions. 'Fine. Look, I'll meet you later by the press room. I must change now.'

As he turned to go into the weighing room the jockeys were coming out for the next race. Willie Angell swore loudly as he shoved James out of his way.

On the way back from the racecourse James tried without success to contact the Chief Superintendent. Eventually he rang Pale's home number, only to be told that he had gone away on police business and would not be back until the morning. James left his name and said that he would call back and that the matter was urgent.

That night he and Gail found a little bistro in the centre of Liverpool, and for the first time James told her what had happened in the medical room. He had wanted to keep the whole business to himself; he was afraid of putting her in danger. But now he accepted, fully and for the first time, how much he had come to need her support and understanding. Without her help, he didn't think he could carry on.

Gail asked to see the marks on his neck, but he refused.

'I wondered why you were wearing a tie. All rather formal for you, though I could see Mrs Crow was impressed.'

'It's not a pleasant sight. I'm just lucky I had the muffler with me, otherwise old Archie would have seen and that would have meant goodbye to tomorrow's race for yours truly.'

'But who could it have been? Didn't you see anything?'

'You're joking. It all happened so quickly. Whoever it was took a real risk coming in there at that time.'

'Yes, but he could also have known that with the race still going on there was a good chance of not being disturbed. You must have some idea.'

'I can only think of Willie Angell. He virtually threatened me in the changing room before the race; he had the opportunity to slip out the back while they were changing for the next race. And did you see that look he gave me as he came out?' Gail nodded. 'It also ties in with our hunch that he is working for the blackmailer. And at least we know it can't have been Lady Croft or Sir Randolph, because they were with you.'

'As a matter of fact, they weren't. I went up on my own to the roof to watch the race and only met the others on the way to see you.'

James thought for a moment. 'And no doubt Archie had gone off to see if Deep Purple was all right, which left the two of them on their own.'

'But how would they know where the medical room was?'

'It's not very difficult to ask somebody, and after all the Stewards' Room is bang next door. And ...'

'And if your late husband was Senior Steward of the Jockey Club ...' Gail burst in. 'But then that means they must have murdered Sir Denby. No, it's ridiculous. Anyway, it can't explain the tapes in the Marsh case. What reason would they have to blackmail Marsh or bug his conversations?'

James had to agree. The one thing he wished was that he knew for sure whether it was Sir Randolph he had glimpsed in bed with Lady Croft. If so, there would at least be some motive for wanting to get rid of her husband. A thought crossed his mind.

'What's up now?' asked Gail, seeing a wicked look come over his face.

'Nothing. By the way, how do you think Mrs Crow would react if two of her lodgers shared the same bed?'

She looked at him from across the table. His face struck her as particularly handsome in the half-shadow of the flickering candlelight.

'I suspect there would be no bacon for breakfast. Rather a shame we shall never find out.' And she gave him a grin.

Chapter 21

They returned to their boarding house and kissed goodnight on the stairs. James undressed quickly and, before getting into bed, studied the marks on his throat in the cracked mirror above the wash basin. Tomorrow he would wear his muffler when he went to see the course doctor to be passed fit and his throat, in any case, was not the anatomy which would be receiving attention.

He was going through TIMEFORM, trying for the umpteenth time to work out the merits of the opposition in the National when there was a light, almost imperceptible, knock on the door.

'Who is it?' he answered.

'It's me,' came the whispered reply.

Only then did James realise the extent of his

unconscious fear; it had even caused him to lock his door. Easing himself stiffly and carefully out of bed, he walked over and opened it.

Gail was wearing a white cotton night-gown. 'There's something I want you to know.'

'Yes.' He forgot that he was wearing only a striped nightshirt and a matching nightcap which his mother had given him and which he had sentimentally put on that night for luck.

'That I love you.'

She came in, closing the door gently behind her. Their lips met as they moved quietly but not altogether effortlessly into the single creaky iron bedstead.

'Are jockeys meant to do this before a big race?' she asked.

'Only amateurs,' he replied, taking her in his arms.

They woke early and went downstairs to the tiny dining room. Bright sunlight was already streaming through the net curtains, giving life to an otherwise dull and soulless setting. There was only one picture on the wall. According to its title, it showed the members of the Southport Rotary Club enjoying an outing in 1926. On the mantelpiece stood a photograph of Mrs Crow as a young woman, scowling down at a short, timid-looking, moustached man who was presumably her late husband. There was sea in the background and the place looked like Blackpool Pier – just before Mr Crow had decided to cut his losses and leap off, suggested Gail. The door opened from the adjoining kitchen and Mrs Crow appeared, her hair cossetted in a lurid green scarf, a menthol cigarette dangling from the corner of her mouth. That face might not have launched a thousand chips but it still knew how to register outraged virtue.

'Did you both sleep well?'

Gail blushed but James, very pleased with himself,

replied, 'Like a log, thank you, Mrs Crow. And your good self?'

'That surprises me. I thought you must have had a very disturbed night with all that creaking from your bed.'

'Really? You must have been hearing things. We've never slept better. You must give me the name of your mattress maker.'

Mrs Crow slammed down the two plates. Each held a black sausage, an overcooked fried egg, one lonely mushroom, but no bacon.

Gail had been right.

Chapter 22

After breakfast they packed quickly, paid the hovering Mrs Crow, and set off for Aintree. As soon as they came across a public call-box James telephoned Pale's home number, to find that the Chief Superintendent had delayed his return to the evening. His wife suggested that it might be sensible to leave a message. So James rather cryptically suggested that the Chief Superintendent might make enquiries at Wainright's Garage in Little Blenerhassett regarding the body repairs carried out on a car registration number A637 PIP. Mrs Pale made no comment. Her nonchalance implied that such leads were left regularly at the Pale household.

Although it was still early morning, the traffic going to the racecourse was reminiscent of the roads to Epsom on Derby Day. Coaches laden with passengers, crates of beer piled high on the back seats, dominated the procession. Eventually the Morris fought its way into the reserved car park and James and Gail were once more surrounded by the group from the day before. Everyone, and in particular Charlie, Deep Purple's owner, was in high spirits and James received the expected ribbing over his spectacular exit from the Foxhunter's. He declined to show them either his wounded pride or his backside.

Leaving Gail on her second gin and tonic he made his way towards the course and what he hoped would be a brief meeting with the racecourse doctor. He had decided to go and see him before training and was wearing a tie to cover up the marks on his throat. The aching was still there and it was absolute agony trying to swallow. He only hoped it did not affect his breathing during the race when the pressure was on.

At least, he reflected, he was still alive. What's more, he had a girlfriend who was loyal, understanding and affectionate. Add to that the fact that he was about to ride in the greatest race in the world and on a horse which had a good chance of being in the frame, and who would not feel that this particular game was worth the candle? As he passed the entrance gate the first thing to hit him was the smell of frying onions from a nearby hot dog stand, an unwelcome reminder of how hungry he was. He had not eaten any of the delights served up by Mrs Crow. He decided to weigh himself in the changing room, and if he was light enough, have a cup of tea and a biscuit. At least these would lie easily on his stomach.

The entrance was jammed with owners and trainers spilling out of the Red Rum bar and press men interviewing jockeys for a last word on their chances. James literally had to push his way through to the changing room. As he walked under the cream canopy and showed his jockey's licence to the gateman he could see to his right the big crowd which had gathered round the television presenter. The big-race build-up had already begun and soon, no doubt, they would be showing to millions of viewers clips of The Sportsman, while analysing his form and that of his jockey as well. At least it wasn't an obituary, as someone had clearly hoped and intended less than twenty-four hours before.

He turned into the weighing room. Immediately in front of him and screwed to the wall was the only telegram board he had ever seen on a racecourse. It was covered with messages, mostly to jockeys but some also to trainers and even one to a horse. He looked under T, more out of curiosity than hope, and to his astonishment found that someone had telephoned him. He took down the message and ripped it open. It read, 'Next time tell me the make of the car. Pale.'

He was chuckling to himself when he heard someone call out 'James', and looked up to find an all-too-familiar face.

'Tom, what the hell are you doing here? I thought you were avoiding Aintree after yesterday's rodeo act.'

'So did I. You'll never believe it, though. My dear father was so upset by what happened that he went out and bought one of the outsiders for the National for me to ride. It's his way of helping me over my disappointment.'

'Has it got any chance at all?'

'Let's put it this way. The bookmakers are offering a 100 to 1 – no, I lie, 150 to 1 – they've heard yours truly is the jockey. But it did jump safely round some way behind the rest of the field last year. TIMEFORM describes it as one paced although I think half paced would be more accurate a description. And before you say anything, I promise to come nowhere near you today. I really am sorry about yesterday's disaster.'

'Don't worry, it wasn't your fault the rein broke. Just try and steer a straight course today.'

'Who's the message from?'

'A well-wisher. Or at least I think he is. Listen, I'm just going to see the doctor to be given the OK to ride. Why don't we have a cup of tea together after that?'

'Fine. I say, I hope you didn't injure yourself too badly?'

'Only some scraped skin.' James didn't mention the post-race treatment he had suffered.

The medical went well and James moved into the changing room. It was still over an hour and a half to the big race but there was already an atmosphere and tension totally unlike any other race day. Jockeys were everywhere, some chatting and changing while others wandered around collecting signatures on their racecards as souvenirs of the great day. In one corner a group had gathered round one of their number renowned for his impersonations. He was now taking off the television commentators, using the occasional word which would not go down so well with the more sensitive viewers. In among the general fray the valets were struggling to do their job, preparing saddles and sorting out colours. By the exasperated looks on their faces it was a losing battle.

'Will you check my saddle, Ernie?' James asked his man.

'It's all done, Jim. Girth, leathers, orange surcingle. Look on the rack above your peg, next to Chris Dorman.'

'Thanks. Marvellous.'

James gratefully made his way to the tea room where he found Tom eating a chocolate digestive from a freshly opened packet. Another unique Aintree event! This was the first time James had ever seen *chocolate* biscuits offered in a weighing room.

They decided to watch the first race on the television and then go and change. Reaching his peg, James found Chris Dorman, the rider of the favourite Single Man, already in his silks and nervously reading that day's edition of the *Sportsman*. The front page headline, 'SINGLE MAN TO COME HOME ALONE,' seemed only to be adding to his nervousness. As James removed his shirt he was determined that nobody should see the marks on his throat and he turned to face the wall.

Surreptitiously putting on his muffler he caught the eye of the jockey sitting three yards to his left, wearing pink and grey colours. Willie Angell's stare was full of hatred. He was riding Archie Duncan's third string in the race, a very reliable jumper but lacking speed and possibly stamina over the distance. James hoped Willie would be concentrating on the race and not on any of his fellow riders.

The second race had barely finished when the bell rang and the call came for the jockeys riding in the National to get ready. James had just started to put on his helmet when the same official shouted out that Mr Townsend the Senior Steward wanted to have a word with them all. Within a few seconds the hubbub of nervous chatter in the room had given way to silence.

'Jockeys, as you know, the ground is riding fast here today and because of that I would like to plead with you to be sensible and not go too quickly over the first few fences. You all know what happened last year and we don't want a repeat of that.' James recalled the disaster. Fifteen horses had fallen at the first two fences as if someone from the rails was picking them off with a machine gun. 'That's all I've got to say, jockeys, other than to wish you the best of luck and a safe journey.'

The atmosphere was now electric. Jockeys were

175

scrambling to get ready. A couple were searching frantically for their silk riding caps and panicking in case they were late. And to add to the confusion somebody's head lad was shouting for Ernie because the girths he had sent out with his saddle were too long and he needed shorter ones urgently. Everyone was wishing everyone else good luck, though James refrained from shaking Angell's hand. Now was hardly the appropriate moment for a bone crusher.

The short walk to the Paddock became an overland trek as they fought their way through crowds of racegoers clamouring for autographs and superstitious punters wanting to touch their jockeys in the hope that this would bring them luck. As James passed the Red Rum bar a young schoolboy asked him to sign his racecard and he was surprised to see just how much his hand was shaking. Entering the Paddock he soon found the smiling group consisting of The Sportsman's new owner, Sir Randolph Vane and Carlton Williams representing the paper, and Mrs Duncan and her two daughters wearing blue and white scarves to match James's racing colours. Archie soon joined them. He had hardly had time to give James his riding instructions when the bell rang for the jockeys to mount.

The Sportsman had never looked better. He was a big powerful bay with a white fetlock on his rear hind leg and there was no doubt that Archie had him ready to run for his life. Mick helped James into the saddle and as he slipped his feet into the irons, something didn't feel quite right. He thought no more of it in the excitement and tension of the occasion. He adjusted his leathers which seemed slightly longer than usual and then gave the young lad who was holding the horse the signal to lead him round the Paddock and onto the course for the parade.

As they made their way along the narrow pathway which led to the course the huge marquees on the grandstand side gave the setting a truly carnival atmosphere. The Sportsman began to break out in a sweat as they joined the parade, while some of the other horses who had run on the course before and knew what they would shortly be doing were jig-jogging with impatience to be on with the race. Immediately in front of James was a horse called Badger's Mount, a tiny liver chestnut who had run the year before and fallen at Becher's Brook on the second circuit. That was clearly an experience he had not forgotten, as he was now white with sweat and prancing about like a circus horse. James told the lad to keep The Sportsman well back. That kind of anxiety was infectious and he didn't want his mount becoming upset and starting to lose energy even before the race had started.

As the commentator called out the names and numbers and it came to his turn, James could feel the eyes of all the spectators on the course and millions of viewers at home boring into him. He wondered whether Pale would take time off to watch the race or whether at this very moment he was pursuing his enquiries at Wainwright's Garage.

The lead horses now turned to make their way down to the start: the top weight Ebony Eyes, then the favourite Single Man, the grey Catcher and his own choice as likely winner, Flanneller. He waited a few seconds before letting The Sportsman go, and cantered down past the County Stand towards the first fence, to give the horse a good look at what lay ahead. To do this, they passed under the starting wire and as they approached the Melling Road with its covering of black grit The Sportsman suddenly jinked his head down and stuck his toes into the ground. James would have stayed on but for his leathers snapping, throwing his weight

E.—9

177

forward and his left leg around under the horse's neck. For a split second he thought he might still be able to stay in the saddle but as he flung his hand out to grab some mane the horse side-stepped to the right, dropping his jockey awkwardly on the base of his spine into the cool black grit. To add injury to insult The Sportsman then kicked him on the ankle before galloping off to join the other horses by the first fence.

The humiliation of the fall took James's mind off his injury. Fortunately one of the other jockeys had grabbed hold of The Sportsman's reins and as he jogged down to collect him James cursed Ernie out loud. If this was his idea of a practical joke ... He had asked him specially to check the leathers.

One of the groundsmen was now leading the horse towards him, a broken leather in his other hand. Happily his action showed there was nothing wrong with the animal. The Sportsman had clearly mistaken the black road for an enormous ditch and thought better of trying to jump it.

But what about the leather? One glance was enough to show James that it had been tampered with. At the point where it folded for the stirrup iron to rest, someone had scored a deep cut and the frayed bit which had snapped was little more than the width of two sheets of newspaper. This certainly wasn't Ernie the valet's work.

He returned to the start to find an anxious Archie waiting to see if they were all right and Mick dancing about with a new set of leathers. These he speedily threaded through the irons and then back through the two holes on either side of the saddle where they attached to the tree.

James realised that if this had happened at the first fence there would have been a very nasty accident. With barely time to remount and to adjust his goggles

178

he heard the starter call the horses to line. There was a bunch of jockeys jostling for position on the inside and James was thankful that he had made up his mind to hunt round the first circuit and ride a race on the second. With horses whipping round and jockeys screaming to the starter to hold on, the butterflies in his stomach were beginning to run riot. At least he now only had the course to beat.

Suddenly, and to a huge cheer, the tapes were up and they were off. James could not believe the pace at which they galloped towards the first fence – the Senior Steward's words of warning were now like smoke in the wind. By the time they had crossed the Melling Road, The Sportsman was ignoring his rider's efforts at restraint and had, it was evident, no intention of letting up. James recognised that if they attempted to jump at this speed they really would be courting disaster and with all his strength he made a concentrated effort to force the half ton of animal below him to slow up and steady itself.

Just as he took what should have been the necessary tug on the reins he felt someone's hand grab hold of his right stirrup and pull it back over his foot. He had no time to see the face which went with it but the flash of pink and grey colours told him enough.

There was no time to think now, as he galloped at nearly 30 mph towards an enormous fence with his foot stuck through his iron. Instinct told him to kick his left foot out of its iron so that at least his legs would be gripping at even length to give himself a chance of staying on. The Sportsman, blissfully unconcerned about his rider's predicament, flew the fence but pecked slightly on landing, shooting James up his neck.

With no irons to pull against he was now slowly losing the battle to stay on. The stirrup round his right leg pulled tight over his calf muscle and he knew that when he hit the fast-moving ground he would be dragged along like a rag doll by that stirrup, and, even worse, trampled on by the horses following.

They had barely gone two furlongs. The Sportsman was as fresh as could be and was bound to continue after the rest of the field. And if James wasn't dead by the next obstacle he certainly would be after it. The new leathers would not break, so the best he could hope for was that his leg would be pulled off before his body crashed into the next fence.

James now knew why something had felt strange when he first sat in the saddle in the Paddock. These weren't his irons at all; they were much larger. If the leathers had not snapped before the start he would be on the ground already.

His hold on the rein was just losing its battle with its body-weight when a hand grabbed underneath his right hip and lifted him just long enough to allow him to put his left arm back over the horse's withers and pull the rest of his body back into the saddle.

'I owed you that,' he could hear Tom's voice shouting. He didn't have time to thank him, as they were now only fifty yards from the second fence and facing a repeat of the previous one. Holding both reins in one hand he fought to maintain some sort of control while he leaned down to his right to try to free his leg from its noose. The action of gripping so tightly to stay on was expanding his calf muscle and compounding his problem. Six strides away from the fence he made a conscious effort to relax the lower half of his body for a split second while he jerked the iron downwards. It worked. The iron was now around his ankle and although he was still a long way from being safe there was a chance that if he fell off, his foot would come out of it. The Sportsman took off and James grabbed his mane in both hands and stuck his legs like limpets round his side. Luckily the shock of nearly falling at the first had taught the horse a lesson, and instead of jumping the fence as if it was a hurdle he got in close to the bottom, arched his back and jumped gracefully and properly. James landed on the other side in almost the same position as on take off.

The instant The Sportsman's feet came into contact with the ground James reached down again and pulled the iron back over his foot. He was now free, but there was no time to enjoy the feeling as the horrendous third now loomed with its enormous ditch and square-cut top.

James bent one leg, then the other, and slid both feet back into their respective irons. He had just enough time to shorten the reins and balance himself.

The Sportsman was a quick learner. He had the fence weighed up long before his jockey and adjusted his stride for take-off without James moving. In the last two strides he just lowered his head for balance and then popped over effortlessly. James patted him gratefully on the head to let him know how clever he was, but such praise was unnecessary. His ears were now pricked and his mind was on the next fence to be conquered.

At a quick glance James reckoned that they were about three-quarters of the way down the field and some ten places further back than he had planned. He told himself not to panic and to remember his pre-race resolution to hunt round the first circuit.

The jangle of irons touching together after each of the first three fences was a sure sign of fallers and he wondered whether the jockey in pink and grey was among them. He hoped not, as he had a score to settle, and what more fitting place than on the course itself. He was tired of his role as the eternal victim.

The next two fences were like kids' stuff, but as they

jumped Becher's, both horse and rider had a salutary reminder that this was the toughest race in the world and that any complacency would be punished. Just as they landed, a faller staggered to its feet and stood up directly in their path. They hit the bewildered animal just behind its loins, causing it to lose balance and fall over again. The sudden impact all but brought The Sportsman to a standstill and, for a ghastly moment, James found himself a lot closer to the horse's ears than he would have liked.

Using all his strength he managed to wriggle back into the saddle and urging The Sportsman back into his stride he sought to make up the precious ground which had again been lost.

There was now no time to be cautious. Having jumped the next fence successfully he switched to the inside as they approached the Canal Turn. He left just enough room to jump it on the angle and now as they galloped towards the Melling Road to rejoin the racecourse proper they were beginning to catch up with the leaders who were taking a short breather. After jumping the last before the road and beginning the long run to what would be the penultimate fence on the second and final circuit, James looked up to see where the fancied runners were.

He had barely lifted his head when The Sportsman veered violently to his left as a horse cannoned into his right shoulder.

Instinctively James jerked on the right reins and only narrowly avoided galloping headlong into the brick pier that was supporting the iron gates beside the road. The outside of his left stirrup iron grazed the corner of the brickwork as they flashed back onto the course. The jockey in pink and grey certainly hadn't fallen. Willie Angell was far too good a rider for that. He'd merely sat in behind James waiting for another opportunity to kill him and once again had come dangerously close to doing so.

Willie was now a couple of lengths ahead of him and although James could guarantee his own safety by staying behind him he still wanted to win the race. He decided to bide his time and wait for a suitable opportunity to pass and, if possible, take his revenge.

The Sportsman was now going easily and hopped effortlessly over the next two fences in front of the stands. At the dreaded Chair he shuffled around a loose horse that had refused right in front of him, and as they landed safely over the other side James caught sight of three jockeys curled up like hedgehogs on the ground. The rider of Ebony Eyes was one of them, which meant one horse the less to worry about. As they jumped the water and turned left-handed to begin the second circuit, James could pick out the colours of Flanneller, Single Man, and Catcher, all in a bunch at the front of the field twenty lengths ahead of him. The horses immediately around him were clearly feeling the strain and now it was a question whether he could successfully pass Willie and catch the leading group.

At the next fence he took a tighter hold on the reins and squeezed The Sportsman between his legs. There was no other feeling in the world like it, he thought, as the horse lengthened his stride and sent a feeling of power and balance through his rider. What a magnificent creature – so strong, so brave and always so trusting, jumping fences when the other side was unknown territory. The horse's power and confidence seemed limitless; he took off whenever James asked him to and landed so far the other side of Becher's that he didn't even notice the drop.

They passed Willie on the inside as they approached the Canal Turn but by the look the Ancient Mariner gave James it was obvious that they would not be allowed to jump the fence alone. As they took off James went as if to cut off the corner but at the last moment checked and carried on for a few yards before pulling on the reins and slowing down to turn left. Willie's horse was not so lucky and galloped relentlessly towards the corrugated iron fence which separated the course from the canal. James glanced over his shoulder to see Willie's animal veer away at the last moment, hurtling his jockey through the air and into the fence at thirty miles an hour. James could hear his screams of agony, and looked around to see the Ancient Mariner rolling in pain on the ground as two St John's Ambulance men rushed to his assistance.

There were now only eight horses ahead of them and judging by the way five of the jockeys were pushing their mounts along there were only three seriously left in with a chance. There was still a mile to go and James knew that The Sportsman was never going to go any quicker. However, he could gallop on relentlessly at his present pace. Two of the strugglers fell at the next, Valentine's Brook, and by the time they had crossed the Melling Road for the last time James had moved up to fourth. They had passed the Catcher, who clearly had run out of steam, and now there was only Flanneller, Single Man, and one other which he did not recognise, ahead of them. Those three were playing cat and mouse with each other, frightened to make the first and final thrust for home in case it gave the others the psychological advantage of having a lead.

Flanneller's jockey could wait no longer and suddenly kicked for home. By the second last and with the vast crowd already roaring him home he had pulled two lengths in front of Single Man. James was now near enough to recognise the third horse – or rather, its jockey. Even Banker had finished fourth in last year's race but had not run at all that season because of injury.

His legs were now beginning to feel weak from the effort of trying to keep The Sportsman in touch and his lungs were burning as he searched desperately for breath. He headed The Sportsman towards a hole in the fence where somebody had crashed through on the first circuit and as the horse took off and jumped through the gap he snatched a much-needed mouthful of air to give him the necessary strength to urge the animal on.

All four horses had landed safely and as they galloped towards the last Even Banker looked to be going better than the leader who was gradually but surely coming back to them. The Sportsman now made his only error in jumping but this was a moment when James could not afford to lose an inch, let alone a length. As he gathered the horse up again and set off on the long gruelling run in to the line he realised that, ironically, the mistake had given The Sportsman a chance to snatch a breath.

By now Even Banker was beginning to edge in front of Flanneller, with Single Man dropping behind. And as they reached the elbow where the chase course went back onto the hurdle course for the finish, the two leaders went straight down the middle.

It was just the luck James needed. With only two hundred yards to go The Sportsman was legless and galloping from memory. As they passed the elbow, James pulled him to the left, causing him to change legs and lead with his left instead of his right. With the fresh leg taking over James threw his last, tiny, painful reserves of oxygen into pushing him forward.

Slowly, with the rail on his left to keep him straight, The Sportsman started catching up on the two ahead. With fifty yards to the line James could sense the others falter and with a final flurry of arms and heels – he had dropped his whip at the first – he almost physically lifted the gallant horse over the line.

They had won!

Yet such was his exhaustion he could hardly breathe or hear the roar of the crowd.

James witnessed the scene in the winner's enclosure, to which he and the The Sportsman were led back through a jubilant crowd, in a state of shock. Sir Randolph, Lady Croft, Archie Duncan and his family, and The Sportsman's new owner and his valiantly overdressed wife were all there to greet the victorious horse and rider.

With one last effort he managed to dismount, unsaddle and pose for a stream of photographs before heading towards the weighing room. It was a struggle to push his way through the crowd. The whole world, it seemed, wanted to say 'Well done!' and to pat him on the back. As he flopped onto the scales, even the usually dour Clerk of the Scales managed a smile and said, 'Good show, Thackeray!'.

As an amateur, James's success did not have the same impact among the other jockeys as if the race had been won by a professional, but he was touched by the way in which, to a man, they came up and congratulated him. 'Get the champagne, son!' shouted one of the more senior riders. It was customary for any jockey winning a valuable race to buy a crate of champagne for the other jockeys to enjoy, and, before he was hauled outside for the ritual interviews, James asked the tea man to go and buy a crate of bubbly and fetch a couple of dozen glasses. Looking round he saw Tom sitting on his own in a corner like one savouring an escape from death. He walked over and shook him by the hand. 'Thanks, Tom. I reckon you saved my life out there.'

'My pleasure. Made my last ride a memorable one. I can now hang up my boots.'

'Did you finish?'

''Fraid not. Brought down at Bechers second time

around, but both horse and rider, as you can see, are doing fine.'

As he emerged from the weighing room, James was called by the interviewer to step in front of the camera. A cheer went up. He was beginning to have difficulty swallowing again and he hoped that he could get away with short answers to the usual questions of what he had had for breakfast, and whether the race had gone according to plan. He chose not to mention either Mrs Crow's *haute cuisine* or Willie Angell's antics. The finish of the race was played over to him and he was asked how he felt. He took the chance to praise The Sportsman's courage, his trainer's skill, and the generosity of his employers in giving him the ride. From there it was on to the huge press conference held in a large room behind the Red Rum bar. All the racing correspondents had gathered there, and were now firing questions at him in the desperate search for a quotable remark for the next day's copy. James did his best not to disappoint them. He was well aware of the fact that next year he would be one of their number again.

Soon the ordeal was almost over and after one last interview for American television, he returned to the weighing room to change. All he wanted now was a cup of sweet tea, and for once the champagne had no appeal. In a daze, he dressed and walked outside. There, waiting for him, a huge grin on her face, was Gail. 'We're off to the Adelphi!' she said, grabbing his hold-all. 'We've taken over Archie Duncan's room and you're going to have a good night's sleep before we drive back to London. By the way, you were wonderful!'

James slept while she drove them back to the hotel, and his next memory was waking up the following morning with Gail beside him, and every Sunday paper scattered around on the bed. As he lay with his head on the pillow, she read out the headlines and showed him the photographs which covered every back page. With the winner's prize money, Archie was now certain to fulfil his ambition to be a leading trainer and the photograph of a jubilant Sir Randolph suggested that he had no regrets in giving The Sportsman away as a prize. The publicity and extra sales as the paper ran the exclusive story of 'How I Won The National' by James Thackeray would be more than adequate compensation.

Gail was reading out loud from one of the papers when she came to a passage subtitled 'Jockey's Serious Injury'.

The words beneath it ran:

But for one jockey this has been the National he'll want to forget. Willie Angell, the 34-year-old Wantage-based jockey, took a crashing fall at the Canal Turn fence when his mount, Young Lochinvar, failed to negotiate the turn. Willie, who was thrown against the corrugated iron fence which separates the course from the river, is now in Liverpool Infirmary with a badly broken leg and a broken collar bone. He will not be able to ride again this season.

James did not pretend to be upset by this information and Gail was in consequence more than a little surprised when he suggested going to visit 'poor old Willie' in hospital that morning before driving back to Lambourn to join in the celebrations which traditionally occur when the winning horse returns to his stable.

Willie was on his own in a side room off the main ward and anyone seeing James and Gail arriving with

armfuls of pink roses and bunches of black grapes
would have mistaken them for close friends or relatives.
James suspected that none of the former category
existed for Willie Angell and from what he had heard of
Mrs Angell she was probably propping up a bar
somewhere and moaning about her problems.

Peering through the small circular window let into
the sick room door they glimpsed Willie propped up in
bed reading a copy of the *News of the World*. He was
covered in bandages and his right leg was suspended in
the air with weights and pullies. Instructing Gail to
keep guard outside, James slipped in and greeted his
'old friend'.

'Hello, Willie. Pleased to see me?'

Willie put down the paper and looked up with an
expression in which incredulity battled with alarm.

'What the bloody hell are you doing here?' he
managed at last. 'Get out or I'll call the nurse.'

His hand reached for the bell which rested on the
table to the right of him and which James deftly moved
just out of his reach.

'Willie, you disappoint me. I thought you'd be
pleased to see a friend and talk over the race.'

'Cut it out, Thackeray. You're going to regret this.
I've got nothing to say, so get out.'

'No dice, old son. Sorry. Not till you've answered
some questions.'

Willie's mouth opened but the expected abuse failed
to emerge. Instead he just stared at James.

'That's better. Now, who planted the bug in Marsh's
yard? You worked for him, so you should know. And I
want an answer.'

Willie still said nothing. His eyes narrowed
unpleasantly as he watched James take the few steps to
the foot of the bed.

'Secondly, did you know who was trying to

blackmail Sir Denby Croft?'

This question brought from Willie a rather feeble attempt at a punch. James took a small step backwards and grinned.

'Thirdly, who else apart from you knew that Archimedes was going to win that day at Newbury?'

'Just bugger off, I said.'

'Not very original, Willie.'

The injured jockey made an attempt to return to his paper. James snatched it away, with a brisk, insulting flourish, and tossed it into a corner of the room.

'Fourthly, did you run over Paddy Develera? Fifthly, did you kill Eric Soper at Fulham Broadway and if so on whose instructions? And sixthly – and I'm sure you'll be pleased to hear lastly – was it you who tried to strangle me at the races on Friday? You have fifteen seconds, Willie, starting from – now.'

The quiz game parody seemed to go down like a lead balloon, the contestant's expression indicating that he did not intend to score high points. When he had counted fifteen James walked slowly to the foot of the bed. Willie's alarmed look returned.

James picked up the hospital notes and shook his head as he read them.

'Good progress so far, Willie old son. Congratulations! What a shame you are just about to go into a sudden and possibly irreversible decline.'

'You bastard. I'll ...' But Willie had hardly had time to open his mouth before James grabbed the weight at the bottom of the bed and started pulling down. The patient let out a scream of agony.

'What's going on?' asked Gail, putting her head round the door. 'Willie not feeling comfortable?'

'No, he's fine. He was just cheering my victory. Knock if you see anyone coming.'

'Let go, you bastard.' Willie's snarl was now turning

into a whine.

'Not till you've answered my questions.'

For a few seconds Willie put up a last feeble show of resistance, clenching his fists to fight the pain, sweating and turning pale.

'All right,' he gasped finally. 'I'll tell you. No, I didn't push your friend. And I didn't try to strangle you yesterday. I telephoned that creep of a stable lad but I didn't run him over.'

'Why should I believe you?'

'Please yourself. I'm not a killer — yet. But if ever I have an opportunity to fix *you* …'

James disregarded this threat. 'And the bug in Marsh's yard? Who planted that?'

'I did, two years ago, when he sacked me as his stable jockey.'

'To spite him?'

'You bet.'

'Who put you up to it?'

'The same person …' By now the pain in Willie's leg was becoming unbearable. He would have screamed again if he hadn't been afraid of a clout on the head from James. And James's expression showed he had no intention of letting up.

'Go on, Willie. The same person who …?'

'Made me telephone Sir Denby at his club. Made me play him the recording — the one of him giving instructions to go easy on that horse of his.'

'And who was that?'

James increased his pressure on the weight a fraction more and Willie started to groan.

'It was, it was — *aagghh*!'

Gail's head came round the door.

'Quick! There's a doctor and nurse coming this way.'

With a grim face James released the pressure and moved towards the door. A youthful-looking doctor and a pretty nurse came in and he turned to Willie with a well-improvised smile.

'Nice seeing you, Willie. Get well soon. All the lads send you their best. Mustn't tire the patient, must we, doctor?'

The young medic beamed and Gail could not resist asking, 'Well, how's he doing then, doctor?'

'It was a nasty knock he took, but we'll soon have him on his feet again. He's strong and fit. That's the main thing.'

'I'm so glad. We've just been telling him to rest up. You know, take the – er – weight off his feet. We wouldn't want you to have a relapse, would we, Willie darling?'

And with a last cheerful wave they were out of the door, down the corridor, and going like the clappers for the car.

Chapter 23

In the office on Monday morning there were two
messages on James's desk. One said that Chief
Superintendent Pale had just phoned and would James
ring him back as soon as he got in. The other was an
invitation: Sir Randolph was asking Gail and himself to
a celebration party at Raleighs on Saturday night.
James thought of Gail and the four-poster bed and his
eyes lit up. He also thought of Clarissa Croft. Would
she, he wondered, once more be among the guests? On
balance, he decided that Willie Angell had probably for
once been telling the truth during their little talk at the
hospital. If so, that narrowed the suspect list even
further. But equally Willie would have reported James's
visit and his life would be even more at risk than before.

A plan had now formed in his mind and he had

decided to make one or two enquiries during the week to see if his suspicions were justified. His first step was to go and see Mrs Lynn, Sir Randolph's ageing but ever-faithful secretary. It was rumoured that she knew more details about her employer's private life than Relish, his other main confidante, and that at least one Fleet Street daily had offered her a fortune for her kiss-and-tell memoirs. Fortunately she had always shown a motherly interest in James, the more so since she had discovered that her sister had attended his late father's church. James now hoped that if he turned on the old charm he might manage to wheedle out of her the guest list for Saturday night and the full name and London address of a certain curvaceous Peruvian.

Daphne Lynn, or Vera as she had affectionately been nicknamed by the staff, was reading that morning's edition of the *Sportsman*. The centre pages, which were folded open on her desk, were covered with photographs of the race, and in the middle of them was a picture of Archie Duncan and the winning owner holding a trophy aloft. On one side of them, beaming, stood Archie's step-daughters in their blue scarves to match The Sportsman's colours, and on the other, Sir Randolph.

'Why aren't you in this picture, James?' asked Vera. 'Or had you done your bit by then and been relegated to the weighing room?'

'I'm afraid there's no trophy or anything for the winning jockey, but that doesn't matter. The fun is in the winning! Can I look at that picture for a moment? I haven't had time to read through the paper properly this morning.' James took the paper from her and studied the photographs intently for a few seconds.

'What's the matter?' quipped Vera. 'Taking a shine to those two girls? A bit young for you I'd have thought!'

'Do you think so? Actually I was looking at their stepfather holding that trophy and for a moment an idea occurred to me.'

'Be careful James. On this paper, ideas can seriously damage your health! Come on, I'm busy. This isn't just a social visit, is it?'

'How *did* you guess? Vera, it's about this party old Randy's giving on Saturday. Who else is going to be there?'

'Don't be nosey. Wait and see! That'll be far more fun!'

'The Duncans, I suppose.'

'Possibly.'

'Carlton Williams?'

'Could be.'

'And Lady Croft, of course?'

'Perhaps.'

'Why all the secrecy? I'm going to know on Saturday, so why not tell me now?'

'Because I am employed as a confidential secretary and if by some chance the guest list slipped out and featured in a gossip column this week I should be for the high jump.'

'Oh, Vera, you know me. I'm as silent as the tomb. It's just that Gail's rather nervous about the occasion and if she was prepared a bit ...'

'Oh, well, I might just possibly ...'

'I'm sure she'll get on well with that nice Puerto Rican girl.'

'Dolores Sanchez, you mean? She's not Puerto Rican, she's Peruvian, and she's a right little ... But I'd better not tell you what I know about *her*. That really would be something for the gossip columnists. Anyway, what makes you think she's going to be there? Now, go on with you, I'm busy.'

'But she will be, won't she, Vera? I can tell it by your

face. You're an angel, anyway.'

It took a couple of phone calls, one to the *Tatler* and one to *Harpers and Queen*, on both of which James had what might loosely be called former girlfriends, to discover Dolores Sanchez's London address. Tomorrow, he decided, he would pay her a visit and ask her the kind of question that no sensible young man with the good of his career in mind would dream of putting to anyone about his employer.

That evening, after a wet day's racing at Windsor, James went round to see Pale at the yard. The Chief Superintendent did not congratulate James on his win in the National, nor did he even seem particularly interested in the attack on him in the ambulance room. He perked up slightly when James, with a flourish, showed him the piece of leather the attacker had dropped on the floor, but then relapsed into gloom and dampingly remarked that it was unlikely, anyway, to reveal fingerprints. He did concede that the visit his men had made to the garage at Little Blenerhassett had not proved unproductive, but then again, as he was sure James would agree, the mere fact that a green Bentley had had repairs done to its offside wing shortly before Christmas did not necessarily mean there was any connection with Paddy's death.

James now told him about his visit to Willie in hospital. Pale was not impressed by the results. 'The man's a born liar. He's the type that can't lie straight in bed.'

'Well, he can't at the moment, that's for sure,' said James. 'All the same, I'm convinced that in the somewhat special conditions of our interview he was more or less coming clean.'

'Yes, young man, but what does that lead to? To the fact that the person who bugged Marsh's phone was trying to blackmail Sir Denby? We know that already.'

'Well, there's one thing it tells *me*. This business is not the work of professional blackmailers, but of the home-grown, amateur variety.'

'What makes you think so?'

'Instinct, I'm afraid,' said James, grinning across the desk. 'And something I saw last time I stayed at my boss's house.'

'And what was that? Another little clue you have chosen to keep hidden from me?'

'It's all rather embarrassing. Have you ever watched a couple making love through the keyhole of a door?'

'No, but I can't wait to hear about it.'

James told him. Pale grunted, pretended to make a few notes, and made him repeat the story.

James then suggested a plan of action and to his surprise, the Chief Superintendent agreed to it.

Dolores Sanchez's Mayfair flat was as colourful as its owner. It seemed to James that a regiment of interior decorators must have slaved for months to create its flamboyant effects – and an army of rich admirers must have clubbed together to provide the furniture. She herself was reclining on a red silk sofa, a glass of champagne and peach juice in her hand and – even Gail would have had to admit – looking stunningly attractive. Her low-cut green silk blouse revealed a magnificent pair of lungs and set off her deep, dark complexion.

'Mr Thackeray,' she purred. 'How can I help you? I thought you were truly magnificent on Saturday.'

'Señora, I apologise for coming to see you like this and for being so uninformative on the 'phone. I have a very embarrassing question to ask, but people's lives, and in particular my own, may depend on the answer.'

'But how can I help? Does Sir Randolph know of this visit?'

'No. For reasons which I believe you will understand and accept, I have come here on my own initiative. And,' he added, suddenly dropping the attempt at pomposity, 'if you tell him, I shall lose my job.'

She laughed. 'How wonderfully dramatic! Go on, tell me what this is all about.'

'O.K.,' said James. 'Here goes. Do you remember the night I came and stayed at Raleighs?'

'Very well. Sir Randolph is the most wonderful host, although I didn't like that Clarissa Croft woman. She's a bitch!'

A touch of jealousy here, thought James. 'Well, what I wondered, what I wanted to ask you, was ... who did you spend the night with?'

Dolores looked at him in utter amazement for what seemed an eternity. Then she flung back her head and roared with laughter. 'I do see now why you shouldn't ask Sir Randolph, or Sir Randy as your newspapers call him. Darling, I will be honest with you ...'

When he left Dolores' flat some twenty-five minutes later, and made his way across Berkeley Square, James had a new spring in his step. Now only one more interview lay ahead of him before, he firmly believed, all the answers would be in his hands. It would, however, be a much less pleasant meeting than the one he had just concluded.

Chapter 24

Morton Marsh was not pleased to see James and Gail. Arriving on his doorstep the next afternoon, they gazed with dismay at his derelict yard and the 'For Sale' notice outside the house, both painful evidence of the ruin of his career. The owner appeared, unkempt, ill-shaven, and smelling slightly of drink.

'What the hell are you doing? I told you when you phoned this morning that I had no intention of talking to you. In fact, Thackeray, I have no intention of seeing you or if possible hearing about you ever again. Now, leave or I'll call the police.'

'Mr Marsh, I fully understand your feelings towards me. All I want now is some help from you in unmasking the people who bugged your phone. At least let me come in and tell you what I have found out.

f at the end you want me to leave, I will, I promise.'

'I said no and I mean no. Don't you people have any feelings?'

Gail now stepped forward. 'Mr Marsh. Three people have already been killed and on Friday someone tried to murder James.'

'I don't believe you.'

'Go on, show him the marks.'

James undid his collar and tie to reveal the red weals surrounding his neck.

'I'd say you had it coming to you.'

'Maybe I did. But don't you want to get even with those who ruined your career?'

Marsh wavered.

'Please, Mr Marsh,' implored Gail.

'All right. Come in. But if I decide you have to go, you go at once. Is that clear?'

The house was as depressing inside as out. It appeared that Marsh now lived there on his own. Dirty cups and plates littered the sitting room. James felt a momentary sense of guilt that he had broken this once successful man.

'Get on with it then,' grunted the former trainer.

'Mr Marsh, I believe that whoever sent me those tapes had been bugging your house for some time for the purpose of obtaining information about your horses.'

'That theory's not new. The police said after the trial that they believed I'd been blackmailed. I told them it was rubbish.'

'You agree they found the bug?'

'Yes. What does that prove?'

'I now know who put it there. Willie Angell.'

'Angell! That slivering little bastard! I chucked him out of this yard because he was so crooked.'

James decided that this was not the best moment to

bring up Marsh's own track record. 'What I couldn't get out of Angell is who put him up to it. But I know that whoever murdered Denby Croft that Friday at Newbury races also knew that your horses were going to run well that day. Can you recall having any conversations about your horses that morning or the night before?'

'Let me think. That was the day before the Hennessy, wasn't it? Yes, I remember that Menelek Forever won for me and I'm All Right Jack was touched off in a photograph. Should have won, but the jockey got caught napping.'

'That's them.'

'I fancied them both a lot that day, and the night before, I phoned Cogan ...'

'The commission agent?'

'... and told him to put a couple of thousand on each of them for me.'

'So if someone had been listening in to your phone calls, they would have known all about that?'

Marsh nodded.

'Where is the phone you used?'

'In the old study.'

'Can we go and have a look at it? I've got an idea. Gail, do you mind waiting here for a moment?'

'What do you want that tape recorder for?' asked Marsh.

'It saves me making notes. Don't worry.'

Ten minutes later, they reappeared. The trainer had mellowed in his attitude and even offered them a cup of coffee, which, after a glance at the state of the kitchen, they politely declined. As he saw them to the car, his last words to James were, 'Fix the bastards!'.

'Who was he referring to?' asked Gail, as they drove away.

'You'll soon see,' James replied.

Chapter 25

Saturday started badly, with a letter from James's bank manager, a balding meglomaniac in the depths of Hampshire. Although it ended respectfully its tone was the reverse, and James now realised that you had to owe truly astronomical sums of money before you were treated with anything approaching deference.

The only other offering from the postman was a letter from the head of the boarding school where his young sister was a pupil, announcing a sudden and unforeseen increase in fees, to take effect from the coming term. Now it really was imperative that James should win his bet on the naps table and, as Gail drily remarked, live long enough to collect it.

Fortunately, after a lean spell in the days running up to the National meeting, he had hit a purple patch and every horse he napped was skating home. His selections were now showing a subtantial profit to a pound stake and only one other tipster, Captain Pundit of the *News*, was ahead of him. James was confident that his selection would win at Newbury and since he had been given a certainty for Wincanton on Tuesday, the last day of the competition, his chances of winning the naps trophy and therefore the bet were high. By a pleasant irony, Tuesday's certainty was owned by the managing director of Sevier's, the bookmakers who had laid him the bet. He looked forward to seeing that grasping gentleman's face as he wrote out to James a cheque for sixteen thousand pounds. He was now glad that he had paid the betting tax up front.

At Newbury his selection coasted home by two lengths and having cheered this success he and Gail drove on to Gloucestershire where they changed at her parents' house before travelling over to Raleighs. The party was due to begin at eight o'clock, and as the Morris trundled up the long drive they sang along to the Stevie Wonder tape which Archie Duncan's stepdaughter Clare had lent them, while poor old Elgar was relegated to the back seat. Judging by the number of cars in the drive most of the other guests had already arrived and James parked the old Morris beside a gleaming green Bentley.

'I think I could just about adjust to one of those,' remarked Gail, patting its long bonnet.

'You shall have one, my darling. Remind me to call the bank manager first thing on Monday morning,' replied James, squeezing her arm and leading her towards the house.

From the noise in the background when Relish opened the door it was clear that the party was already well under way.

'Might I suggest that I show Sir and Madam where

their rooms are before fetching their cases from the car?' asked the unsmiling butler.

They agreed that this would be best. James was glad to see that he had been given his old room, but his dreams of a riotous night together tumbling in the ample four-poster evaporated as Relish, taciturn as ever, led Gail off and up another flight of stairs. Perhaps just as well after all, reflected James, who had plans for the evening that Gail was not to know about.

In the drawing room the atmosphere was even more festive than usual, the clothes more dazzling, the conversation more unrestrained. Most of the faces were familiar to James and Gail: there were the Duncans of course, Archie, his wife and the two girls; Carlton Williams and his wife; the deputy editor and his live-in girl friend; and the other directors of the newspaper and their spouses.

'Hey, James!' Dolores's voice rang out from the other side of the room, and she moved across to greet him. Her dress was a shocking pink, its cut an outrageous, even more shocking *décolleté*. She flung her arms round James and kissed him passionately on both cheeks, leaving smears of bright lipstick.

'And you must be James's girlfriend,' she said, turning to Gail. 'He is a very lucky young man, but I must warn you, a very naughty boy with it!' Giving him a pinch on the cheek, she turned away to the next group.

Gail looked frosty. 'And just what did you do with that strumpet when you went to see her?' she asked, when the Peruvian had swept out of earshot. 'I saw the way your eyes were buried in her cleavage just now!'

'Oh, we talked about this and that.'

'Just talked …?'

'Certainly. How dare you impugn the integrity of a journalist?'

'Easily! That woman would eat you for breakfast – a continental one in her case!'

'Look out, here comes Sir Randy.'

The *Sportsman*'s proprietor was looking as dapper as ever in a dark blue velvet smoking jacket. His woven hair boasted not a strand out of place.

'James. Gail. How good to see you both. Let me get Relish to fill up your glasses. We're going to have a hell of a party tonight provided that oaf of an under-butler over there doesn't spill too many drinks.'

They looked across the room to where a podgy middle-aged man in tails was clumsily trying to balance a tray of glasses in one hand while pouring champagne from a bottle in the other. The result was a drenching for the sleeve of Archie Duncan's dinner jacket.

Sir Randolph groaned.

'Cave, my usual number two, is away on holiday, so we had to find this late replacement. Dolores got him from some agency in London but I doubt they will be in business much longer if he's the best they can do.'

James could not restrain his laughter as the stand-in butler dropped his napkin and in bending down to pick it up trod firmly on Lady Croft's left foot. She was plainly not amused and turned angrily away, muttering a complaint to Archie Duncan who stood beside her.

Suddenly Sir Randolph called for silence and when the chatter had died began to speak. 'We are all gathered here tonight to celebrate The Sportsman's achievement in last week's race. It is everyone's dream to be associated with the winner of the National and although I had given away the horse before the race I still felt very much part of his victory. I ask you to join with me now in toasting the health of the two men who made it possible – Archie Duncan, a genius of a trainer, and James Thackeray, a very talented amateur jockey. And finally, let me say a word of thanks to Clarissa

Croft who introduced me to Archie in the first place.'

'Archie Duncan and James Thackeray,' roared the rest of the party as they drank even more champagne.

'And now,' it was Sir Randolph speaking again, 'before we have dinner I should like you all to come through to the library to watch a video of the race.'

As the picture came up on the screen it was as though the guests were back on the racecourse, clapping, cheering, and finally shouting The Sportsman home as he came up on the inside to win on the line.

'A marvellous effort, really, James,' said Carlton, who was standing beside him. 'But lucky your leathers broke before and not during the race and then you had that chap to help you back into the saddle.'

'I know. The gods were with me. Don't you agree?' James answered, turning to Archie on his right.

'Definitely. But I had a few words to say to that valet, I can tell you. He claims it was a freak accident — the sort of thing that happens once in a jockey's lifetime. I said this was once too often.'

'Well anyway,' said James, 'only I was to blame for slipping through my irons during the race. The funny thing is, I had asked the valet to check those leathers specially.'

'I hope you gave him a piece of your mind afterwards. I can tell you, if you had fallen off, I would have horsewhipped the fellow.' Archie's voice was loud with indignation.

'In fact, I was so tired I didn't say anything. I like to think it was just an accident.'

Several guests were asking for the video to be run through again when Relish announced that dinner was served, and the party of twenty-four marched hungrily into the dining room. It was a magnificent and raucous meal. Sir Randolph had lashed out spectacularly on the wine and food, and it appeared that he had even imported a French chef for the occasion. James tucked in with gusto, throwing his former weight worries to the wind. The laughter which filled the room only increased when the temporary butler dropped one of the vegetable tureens and emptied a rather large helping of *mangetout* down the neck of the deputy editor.

By the end of dinner, everyone was in high spirits and when Relish announced that coffee was served in the music room for the ladies, Dolores made Sir Randolph promise that the men would not linger too long over their port. 'Tonight,' she announced. 'I'm in the mood for dancing, so make sure you hurry up!'

The ladies had scarcely departed when Archie Duncan rose to his feet. 'In all the excitement, we have forgotten to congratulate our host on the news of his election to the Jockey Club. Gentlemen, I give you our host.'

It was obvious to the company as they rose to drink his health that the owner of Raleighs was delighted with his new honour.

'For me,' he replied 'this is the realisation of one of my greatest wishes. My one sadness is that a vacancy exists only because of the tragic death of my friend Sir Denby Croft.'

'Tragic indeed,' echoed Archie, who then turned to Carlton Williams: 'I suppose this means fewer attacks on the so-called cabbage-patch kids from now on, then?'

'Not a bit of it!' the editor replied. 'The paper will continue to publish what it believes to be right, irrespective of the pedigree or breeding of the target. Just as we did in the Marsh case – and, if I may say so, I think you're one person who has benefited by that particular policy.'

'I'm sorry. I don't quite follow.' Archie's voice betrayed a touch of anger.

'No offence, old boy. It's just that I understood that quite a few of Marsh's old owners have come to you now.'

Before Archie could comment, Sir Randolph broke in. 'What's happened to that fellow Marsh? Paying the penalty suffered by anyone who takes on the might of the *Sportsman*, I suppose.'

'Not far off it I'm afraid, sir.' It was now James's turn to reply. 'I went down to his yard last Wednesday, and it was really a depressing scene. Of course, all his horses have gone to new stables; the place is neglected and up for sale, and there was no sign of his wife at all. A far cry from you, Archie, only three miles away!'

Archie nodded. 'Yes, it's a frightening thought how fates can change so quickly. Old Marsh was a good trainer in his day.'

'You two will have me crying in a moment!' interjected Carlton. 'Marsh was a crook and he was caught. It's as simple as that.'

'What were you doing visiting him anyway, James?' asked Sir Randolph. 'Not more of that ridiculous sleuthing, I hope?'

'Well ... er ... sort of. I was following up something concerning the Croft murder, something I learnt from a jockey.'

'Which jockey?' asked Carlton. 'Have you been keeping things from your beloved editor?'

James sidestepped the last question and replied, 'Willie Angell. I went to see him in hospital last Sunday to commiserate with him over his fall.'

There was, James felt, a sudden change in the atmosphere in the room.

'But I thought you hated the chap,' remarked Carlton. 'You're always writing rude articles about him.'

'I don't like him much. I think he's crooked and a lot

208

worse. But I felt responsible for his injury, so I decided to take him some flowers.'

'So what did he tell you which necessitated a visit to Marsh?' asked Sir Randolph, puffing on his obscenely large Havana.

'Only that *he* had placed the bug in Marsh's flat, which led to those tapes we received.'

'He did *what*?' It was Archie's turn to sound surprised. 'The scoundrel! He should be drummed out of racing!'

'That's not all he told me, though. He said he placed the bug there some two years ago, but on somebody else's instructions.'

'Well, did he say who?' asked Carlton eagerly.

'No. He was just about to tell me when we were unfortunately interrupted. But he did admit that, on that same person's instructions, he had telephoned Sir Denby at his club, and played him a tape of an incriminating conversation between the Senior Steward and his trainer.'

All eyes turned towards Archie. 'Did you know your phone was being tapped as well, Archie?' asked Sir Randolph. 'I suppose that would include all my calls to you! Oh, dear!'

'Yes, I'm afraid it's true,' said the trainer. 'The police removed the bug a couple of months ago. I've deliberately kept it quiet so as not to upset all my owners. Of course, if anyone tried to use the tapes for any improper purpose at any time, I had arranged with the police to tell them straight away.'

'By that, Archie, I suppose you mean blackmail?' interposed James. 'But I'm beginning to think that whoever listened into Sir Denby's conversations didn't do it merely with the intention of blackmailing him.'

'And just what makes you say that, young man?' The tone of Sir Randolph's voice had suddenly become rather more strident.

'I see it this way, sir. For some reason, somebody – let's call him Mr X – wanted Sir Denby dead. The phone call to his club was to make him think he was being blackmailed, probably by Weatherby. He was then lured to Weatherby's box, believing that the tape or tapes would be handed over for a certain sum of money. In fact, Weatherby knew nothing at all about it, but he was set up to look like the killer, following the incident between himself and Sir Denby at the enquiry. The same Mr X had been taping Marsh's conversations, and the libel action gave him the ideal opportunity to ruin him publicly.'

'Ridiculous!' exclaimed Sir Randolph. 'Other than a blackmailer, who would want to kill old Denby? No, my boy, you're quite wrong there. I think that fall before the National has done permanent damage to your brain. Have another glass of port!' Everyone, including James, laughed.

'I'm convinced they're all linked. Look at this betting slip which I found on the floor of the horse box beside Sir Denby.' James produced a photostat copy of the slip from his jacket pocket and laid it on the table. Sir Randolph, Archie and Carlton got up from their chairs to gather round him. All the others listened intently. 'You see,' continued James, 'of these four, three won and the other was beaten in a photo finish. Menelek and I'm All Right Jack were trained by Marsh.'

'And the other two?' asked Sir Randolph.

'By Archie.'

'I see now,' exclaimed Sir Randolph. 'The same person had obviously bugged both phones and knew they were fancied.'

'So it seems,' continued James. 'But that means that Archie knew that Archimedes was going to win, and told somebody about it. Did you, Archie?'

There was a short silence before the trainer replied. 'The answer is no, and no. I was astonished when Archimedes won. As you must recall, I had another much more fancied runner in the race. So, no, I certainly wouldn't have told anyone, either on the phone or any other way, that I fancied the horse. What about Marsh? Did you ask him the same question about his horses?'

'I did, actually, and after a great deal of cajoling, he became very forthcoming. He did fancy both his runners that day. And the night before, he telephoned his commission agent, Cogan, and told him to place large bets on his behalf – two thousand pounds on each horse!'

'Who rode Archimedes that day, James?' Carlton now asked.

'Have a guess.'

'Not your friend Willie, I suppose?'

James nodded and smiled. 'And that was another question I asked Angell in hospital. He had ridden the horse on its two previous outings, so I asked him who told him to pull it then.'

'Some damned bookmaker, I suppose. That chap will never ride for me again!' stormed Archie.

'No, Willie didn't say. We were interrupted at the vital moment.'

'Have you told the police all this yet, James?' asked Sir Randolph.

'I certainly hope not! He hasn't even told his editor,' quipped Carlton.

'Not yet. I think they still believe there's a gang of murderous blackmailers loose.'

At this point the door opened, and Dolores's head appeared round it. 'Come on, Randolph. We cannot dance on our own, and anyway, where do you hide all your good records? All I can find is Frank Sinatra singing love songs.'

The men rose to their feet, and obediently followed

her into the music room, where they found the Frank Sinatra record playing, while the women stood around drinking and talking. Dolores had already turned the lights down.

'We've gone through all the records. There's just nothing here to dance to,' moaned Clare.

'I've got an idea,' said James. 'Gail, we still have those tapes in the car which Clare lent us for the journey up to Aintree.'

'That's right,' said Clare. 'They're the ones I recorded myself at home on some old tapes. There's one of Stevie Wonder, and one of my own personal greatest hits. Shall I go and get them with you, Gail?'

Within five minutes, the two girls were back with the tapes. Soon everybody was dancing to Stevie Wonder, and the room shook with noise and body movement. Dolores had dragged Sir Randolph up to dance and was making him boogie, to the delight of the rest of the guests. Sweat was pouring off his brow.

When Stevie Wonder had done his bit, James offered to be the disc jockey and put on the other cassette. The music became louder and louder, faster and faster. Suddenly it stopped. In its place, the sound of men's voices came booming over the loudspeakers. Everybody stood transfixed.

'Hello, is that you, Cogan?'

'Yes, who is it?'

'It's Morton Marsh here.'

'Oh, hello. What can I be doing for you?

'I've got two runners tomorrow at Newbury, Menelek and I'm All Right Jack. Could you put two thousand on each of them for me?'

'Certainly. No problem. Anything else?'

'No, that's fine, thank you'.

The voices ceased as suddenly as they had begun and the pounding music resumed.

The lights came on.

'What the hell is happening?' Sir Randolph pushed Dolores away and walked unsteadily towards the record player. 'Turn that damn music off for a moment.'

James stopped the cassette and looked round the crowded room. It was plain from the expressions on most of the dancers' faces that they were completely baffled. Not so Carlton, however. He had been standing in a corner listening to the music and watching the dancing, a large brandy in his hand.

'That sounded like a conversation between Morton Marsh and his bookmaker,' he now observed. 'And I shouldn't be surprised if it was the one they had the night before the Newbury meeting when Sir Denby was murdered.'

'Is this some kind of a joke, James?' barked Sir Randolph. 'Where did you get this tape?'

James was opening his mouth to answer when there was a loud thud. Clarissa Croft had collapsed onto the floor.

'Quick,' shouted Archie. 'She's fainted. Get some brandy!' He rounded on James. 'I hope you're satisfied with your stupid little prank, Thackeray.'

Within instants the stand-in butler had produced a glass and Gail held Clarissa's head as Mrs Duncan gently poured the spirit down her throat. Archie and Carlton lifted her up and carried her next door to the drawing room where they placed her on a sofa. Ten minutes later Sir Randolph announced that Clarissa was feeling better but had decided to go to bed.

'Good!' said Dolores. 'We can now get on with the party. Put on some more music, James.' Grabbing Sir Randolph, she flung him round the dance floor.

An hour or so later, the party broke up and Gail and James went wearily to their respective beds. The sound

213

of closing doors and padding feet gave way to silence and James began to wonder whether he should creep along the corridor and up the stairs to see Gail. The only trouble was, he could not remember whether it was the third or fourth door along, and he certainly didn't fancy slipping between the sheets with the deputy editor and his girlfriend. With reluctance, he abandoned the idea. Instead, staring at the ceiling, he reflected on the evening's events. Everything which had occurred had confirmed his suspicions and he wondered whether he should make the next move or simply wait. But one thing was clear to him. He had to retrieve that tape and he cursed his luck that no suitable opportunity had presented itself to enable him to do so earlier. There was a real possibility that Clare would ask for it in the morning, and even if she didn't, Gail would probably hand it over. He had better go and get it now.

Putting on his dressing gown, he tiptoed down the stairs, holding on to the bannisters to guide him in the darkness. The door of the drawing room creaked slightly as he opened it, but there was no sound of any movements above. He crossed the room, feeling his way along the edge of the large sofa, and into the music room beyond. He drew the curtains apart to let in the moonlight. The chairs and sofas had been pushed back near the walls to leave room for the dancers. There were several records and cassettes beside the record player, but he soon found the one he was looking for. He held it up and kissed it.

The force of the arm around his throat threw him off balance. Instinctively, he jabbed his elbow into the stomach of his attacker; a gasp and slight relaxation of the grip told him that the blow had registered.

'Turn him round, you fool!' came a voice from the darkness.

Struggling, James was forced to confront the waiting

blade of a knife, and a face convulsed with anger and hatred. He could feel the sweat pouring off his brow.

'Not such a hero now, Mr Thackeray! And not so quick either. As you see, we were ahead of you, and the tape isn't going to do you much good now. Because ...'

There was a click as the lights went on. The hand holding the dagger froze.

'Was this how you killed your husband, Lady Croft?'

James had never been so glad to hear that voice. Standing by the light switch in his butler's uniform of black jacket and striped trousers, Chief Superintendent Pale held a revolver with considerably more dexterity that he had the dinner plates.

'Don't you think you ought to let Mr Thackeray go now, Mr Duncan? Hardly the way for a trainer to treat one of his jockeys.'

Archie Duncan backed away. 'Look, please, it was all her idea.'

'Shut up!' hissed Clarissa.

The Chief Superintendent moved forward to the middle of the room. 'Clarissa Croft and Archibald Duncan, I charge you with the murders of Sir Denby Croft, Eric Soper, Patrick Develera, and with the attempted murder of James Thackeray. I must warn you that anything you say may be taken down and used in evidence against you.'

Chapter 26

James boarded the early morning train for Wincanton in a state of unrestrained optimism. His 'certainty' was running in the second race, a two-mile handicap hurdle, and when – not if – it duly obliged he would be the winner of the Naps competition. Even more important, he could look forward to the receipt of a fat cheque from his bookmaker.

Settling into his seat in the breakfast car he was soon joined by the racing correspondent for the *Post*, known in his tipping capacity as The Sage. He complimented James on his part in solving the Croft murder case, which had made the headlines in yesterday's papers, and asked him what was his final nap of the season.

'I've gone for Euphemism in the second. I reckon it can't be beat.'

'You're right about that, my son. It's a non-runner. Withdrawn late last night with heat in its leg.'

'I don't believe you. It can't be,' said James desperately flicking through his hitherto unopened copy of the *Sportsman* to find the Wincanton card. 'Damn it, you're right. The buggers have fixed me.'

He threw the paper down in a rage, cursing his bookmakers, whom he suspected of having deliberately withdrawn the horse, whom they also owned, when they saw that he had napped it.

'I suppose that means you lose the Naps competition?' asked The Sage.

'I'm afraid it does. Captain Pundit was a pound ahead of me, but as he has gone for an even money shot today, I was confident I would overtake him.'

'Bad luck. Still, there's always next year.'

The Sage could not know that James faced financial ruin. He owed several thousand pounds and could expect little mercy from his creditors. He looked aimlessly out of the window, wondering how he would break the news to his mother, and whether his sister would actually have to leave her school.

Suddenly The Sage exclaimed, 'Hey James! Were you pulling my leg? Look at this story!'

James grabbed the paper. On the front page of the *Sportsman* there was the headline. 'Thackeray's Nap' and below it the announcement: 'Owing to the late withdrawl of Euphemism, James Thackeray's nap today is Eavesdropper, down to run in the 4.15 Drink More Cider Handicap Chase at Wincanton'.

James's soaring hopes collapsed. It was only too clear what had happened. Euphemism's withdrawal must have come in so late that the sub-editor on duty, in order to catch the late edition, had barely had time to substitute another name. He could not be blamed for failing to contact James, who had gone out to the cinema anyway. But equally, he could not be congratulated on the brilliance of his choice. Eavesdropper's form over fences that season had been a series of disasters, and the only reason any journalist would have picked out his name would have been as an intentional pun on the Croft affair.

* * *

The Drink More Cider Handicap Chase had not attracted a high-class field and by the last fence on the far side, an open ditch, three horses had drawn away from the rest. Eavesdropper was one of them. But it was plain to James, as he watched through his binoculars, that his jockey was already having to push the horse along to stay in touch. As they turned towards home, and ran downhill to the next fence, the increase in pace found Eavesdropper falling three lengths behind, and James now sensed that his dream of winning the Naps competition was definitely gone.

A groan went up from the crowd, and James looked up to see that the favourite had made a complete mess of the third fence from home, and had unseated his rider. The new leader had only two fences to jump, but poor Eavesdropper was plodding on, one-paced, making no impression on his lead. As they approached the final fence, the jockey on the leader decided to be cautious and pulled his mount back on his hocks to make sure he jumped properly, and didn't fall. James watched in disbelief as the horse, as sometimes happens, over-reacted, and all but refused.

It took less than a second for the three length advantage to disappear, as Eavesdropper attacked the fence and flew past him in mid-air. Together, the horses battled it out over the short downhill run to the winning post. James's frantic screams of encouragement rose above the noise of the crowd. But as the two runners passed the post together, it looked as though Eavesdropper had been caught and beaten on the nod.

The wait for the photograph seemed interminable, and the result came just as James had resigned himself to defeat. Once again, he had no wish to appeal the judge's decision ...

Chapter 27

That night Gail and James celebrated together at Angelo's. It was almost six months to the day since they'd first sat down to dinner there.

Gail had deliberately kept back her questions about the Croft case until now, when they could feel completely relaxed.

'When did you first suspect that it was Archie and Lady Croft?'

'I became suspicious about her ladyship after I saw her in bed with the man I thought was Sir Randolph. She's a good-looking woman and, as events have shown, had married her husband for his money, but was in no mood to wait for it. When Pale told me it was Sir Randolph who had bought the horse from Weatherby I was convinced that she and my beloved proprietor had dreamt that up as part of their plan to frame the disgraced trainer. No doubt Sir Denby had told her about Weatherby's conduct at the enquiry, and he made an obvious suspect. It very nearly worked.'

'So what made you change your mind about old Randy?'

'Once I realised the extent of Angell's involvement and started thinking about the betting slip. Who knew best of all that Archimedes would win that day? His trainer, of course. Then again, who had a better motive for listening into his biggest rival's phone calls? Right again. And when the trial came on, good old Archie couldn't resist the opportunity to ruin Marsh once and for all.'

'But why should Duncan bug his own phone?'

'Why not? What more simple idea than to bug your own calls in case your owners make an incriminating remark which you can later use against them? In fact, that's just what Archie was able to do with Sir Denby. The last person Sir Denby would suspect as a blackmailer was the other party to his conversations. Then that Friday at Newbury, Sir Denby goes to Weatherby's box expecting to meet the blackmailer and recover the incriminating tape. Why should he suspect that his own wife and trainer have set him up? They follow him there, murder him and return to the course, ready to give each other alibis if necessary.'

'So, Lady Croft was the true villain of the piece.'

'Oh, yes. She was the brains, and delivered the fatal blow. Duncan told Pale that they became lovers on the trip to Hong Kong last year. Ironically, it was organised by the Jockey Club.'

'And Paddy? Why was he killed?'

'He saw Clarissa and Archie go into the horsebox. When he heard of the murder, he put two and two together and tried a little blackmail on his own account.

Silly fool. It cost him his life.'

'But when were you sure it was Archie, and not Randy?'

'I was pretty sure when I saw the photograph of him in Monday's paper holding the National Trophy. It was the first time I had noticed the rings on his left hand. His step-daughters' blue scarves gave me an idea that he might have borrowed one of them for a little trip to Fulham Broadway station, where he expected to meet yours truly. The tweed overcoat made him think it was me, and not poor old Eric, he pushed. Archie says Clarissa made the phone call to the office.'

'How ghastly!'

'The clincher came when I asked Dolores who she spent the night with that time at Raleighs over Cheltenham. Apparently, Sir Randy is well-named. He wouldn't leave her alone all night. She agreed to help me on Saturday night, and hired old Pale as second butler. To his credit, he went along with it, although he was rather dubious. Look, he even sent me round a present. I've brought it along.'

'Oh, good. Do open it!'

James undid the outer wrapping paper, then gave the box to Gail. 'No, you open it for me.'

She opened the cardboard box and from the folds of yet more paper produced a sharp and extremely offensive weapon. She stared at it in alarm. 'Is this his idea of a joke?'

'Let's put it like this,' said James, grinning. 'The Mitcham Machete Mob took it very seriously.'

The sambuccas were not on the house this time, but the two of them still managed to make a good dent in the bottle.

'One last thing. You have to admit it was a stroke of luck finding that recording of Marsh on the tapes we borrowed from Clare. Duncan must have thought they had been rubbed off a long time ago.'

'They were! Clarissa would have seen to that. I recorded that conversation when we went down to see Marsh and he and I went into his office. I thought I did Cogan's voice rather well, didn't you? Clarissa fell for it, anyway. Her so-called faint was well-staged to distract attention.'

It was now Gail's turn to laugh. 'So, what are you going to do with your winnings?'

'After paying off my debts and the school fees, I reckon I'll have about seven thousand over. Do you have any suggestions?' He stretched out his hand to clasp hers, and looked romantically into her eyes.

'That would be enough for a deposit, wouldn't it?' she answered.

'Do you mean on a house together?' At last, James felt, he was about to win the hand of the girl he loved.

'No, you fool! On a racehorse in Ireland!'

All Futura Books are available at your bookshop or
newsagent, or can be ordered from the following address:
Futura Books, Cash Sales Department,
P.O. Box 11, Falmouth, Cornwall TR10 9EN.

Please send cheque or postal order (no currency), and
allow 60p for postage and packing for the first book
plus 25p for the second book and 15p for each additional
book ordered up to a maximum charge of £1.90 in U.K.

B.F.P.O. customers please allow 60p for
the first book, 25p for the second book plus 15p per
copy for the next 7 books, thereafter 9p per book.

Overseas customers, including Eire, please allow £1.25
for postage and packing for the first book, 75p for the
second book and 28p for each subsequent title ordered.